'What you will find, among... alarming evocations of the ... course, more importantly, ... living soul as he confronts a choice between mortal and supernal prizes. In this fine novella Eric Brown joins the ranks of Graham Joyce, Christopher Priest and Robert Holdstock as a master fabulist.'

Paul di Filippo

ERIC BROWN
A Writer's Life

The right of Eric Brown to be identified as the author
of this work has been asserted by him in accordance
with the Copyright, Designs and Patents Act 1988.

First published in Great Britain in 2002 by
Gollancz
An imprint of the Orion Publishing Group
Orion House, 5 Upper St Martin's Lane,
London WC2H 9EA

This edition published in Great Britain in 2003
by Gollancz

A CIP catalogue record for this book
is available from the British Library

ISBN 0 575 07505 8

Typeset at The Spartan Press Ltd,
Lymington, Hants

Printed in Great Britain by
Clays Ltd, St Ives plc

Edwards, Vaughan, (1930–1996?). English novelist, author of twelve novels and two collections of stories. His first novel, *Winter at the Castle*, (1951), received considerable critical acclaim but, like much of his subsequent output, little widespread popularity. Edwards was very much a writer's writer, eschewing the trappings of sensationalism in his fiction and concentrating instead on his own peculiar and unique vision. In book after book, this singular novelist wrote of a rural England haunted by ghosts of the past – both the spirits of humans and the more metaphorical apparitions of times long gone. The novel considered his finest, *The Miracle at Hazelmere*, (1968), tells, in his customary highly wrought prose, the story of William Grantham, an estranged and embittered artist, and his (perhaps imaginary – it is never revealed) affair with the phantom of a sixteen-year-old girl from the Elizabethan period. This novel, in common with the rest of his oeuvre, contains much striking imagery, pathos and a yearning for a long gone era of bucolic certainty. Artists and loners burdened with tragic pasts appear again and again in his writing, and there is speculation that the novels and stories drew much from the author's own life, though, as Edwards was an intensely private person, this has never been confirmed. Critics generally agree that his final novels, the *Secrets of Reality* series, marked the artistic low-point of his career. Though beautifully written, and containing much of ideative interest, the novels, beginning with *Those Amongst Us*, (1990), continuing with *A Several Fear*, (1993), and *The Secret of Rising Dene*, (1996), show an obsessive preoccupation with the arcane, and found only a narrow readership. The series, a projected quartet, was unfinished at the time of the author's mysterious disappearance in the winter of 1996.

From *Encyclopaedia of Twentieth Century British Novelists*, Macmillan, Third edition, 1998.

The above entry was the first mention I had ever heard of the writer Vaughan Edwards. I was surprised that I had never happened upon his work, as I have a pretty comprehensive knowledge of British writers of the last century and especially those publishing after the Second World War. The discovery filled me with a wonderful sense of serendipitous anticipation: there was something about the entry that told me I would take to the novels of Vaughan Edwards. The fact that he was relatively unknown now, and little regarded during his lifetime, gave me the sense that I would be performing a service to the memory of the man who had devoted his life, as the entry stated, to 'his own peculiar and unique vision'. Perhaps what gave me a certain empathy with the novelist was that I too was an unsuccessful writer, the author of half a dozen forgotten novels, as well as over fifty short stories buried away in long-defunct small-press magazines and obscure anthologies.

I showed the entry to Mina. For some reason – perhaps subsequent events have branded the very start of the episode on my consciousness – I recall the night well. It had been a grey, misty day in early November; a gale had blown up after dinner, and now a rainstorm lashed the windows of the cottage, instilling in me the romantic notion that we were aboard a storm-tossed galleon upon the high seas.

Mina was reading in her armchair before the blazing fire. Her favourites were the classic Victorians, the Brontës, Eliot and the rest. Now she laid the well-read paperback edition of *Wuthering Heights* upon her lap and blinked up at me, perhaps surprised at the summons back to the present day.

I set the thick tome on the arm of the chair and tapped the page with my forefinger. 'Why on earth haven't I come across him before?'

She pushed her reading glasses up her nose, pulled a frown, and read the entry. A minute later she looked up, a characteristic, sarcastic humour lighting her eyes. 'Perhaps because he's probably even more obscure and terrible than all those others you go on about.'

I leaned over and kissed her forehead. She laughed. The masochist in me found delight in setting myself up as the butt of her disdain.

I relieved her of the volume, sat before the fire and reread the entry.

Why was it that even then I knew, with a stubborn, innate certainty, that I would take to the works of this forgotten writer? There was enough in the entry to convince me that I had stumbled across a fellow romantic, someone obscurely haunted by an inexplicable sense of the tragedy that lies just beneath the veneer of the everyday – or perhaps I was flattering myself with knowledge gained of hindsight.

Mina stretched and yawned. 'I'm going to bed. I'm on an early tomorrow. Come up if you want.'

Even then, a year into our relationship, I was insecure enough to ascribe to her most innocent statements an ulterior intent. I remained before the fire, staring at the page, the words a blur, and tried to decide if she meant that she wished to sleep alone tonight.

At last, chastising myself for being so paranoid, I joined her in bed. Rain doused the skylight and wind rattled the eaves. I eased myself against her back, my right arm encircling her warm body, and closed my eyes.

· · ·

Though the novels of Daniel Ellis are founded on a solid bedrock of integrity and honesty, yet they display the flaws of an excessive emotionalism which some might find overpowering.

From Simon Levi's review of the novel *Fair Winds* by Daniel Ellis.

But for Mina, I would never have come upon Vaughan Edwards' novel *A Bitter Recollection*. During the month following my discovery of his entry in the encyclopaedia, I wrote to a dozen second-hand bookshops enquiring if they possessed copies of any of his works.

Of the three replies I received, two had never heard of him, and a third informed me that in thirty years of bookdealing he had come across only a handful of Edwards' titles. I made enquiries on the Internet, but to no avail.

I forgot about Vaughan Edwards and busied myself with work. I was writing the novelisation of a children's TV serial at the time, working three hours in the mornings and taking the afternoons off to potter about the garden, read, or, if Mina was not working, drive into the Dales.

It was an uncharacteristically bright but bitterly cold day in mid-December when I suggested a trip to York for lunch and a scout around the bookshops.

As I drove, encountering little traffic on the midweek roads, Mina gave me a running commentary on her week at work.

I listened with feigned attention. The sound of her voice hypnotised me. She had a marked Yorkshire accent that I have always found attractive, and an inability to pronounce the letter *r*. The word 'horrible', which she used a lot, came out sounding like 'howwible'. Perhaps it was the contradiction of the conjunction between the childishness of some of her phrases, and her stern and unrelenting practicality and pragmatism, which I found endearing.

She was a State Registered Nurse and worked on the maternity ward of the general hospital in the nearby town of Skipton. In the early days of our relationship I was conscious, perhaps to the point of feeling guilty, of how little I worked in relation to her. I could get away with three or four hours a day at the computer, five days a week, and live in reasonable comfort from my output of one novel and a few stories and articles every year. By contrast Mina worked long, gruelling shifts, looked after her two girls for three and a half days a week, and kept up with the daily household chores. When I met her she was renting a two-bedroom terraced house, which ate up most of her wage, and yet I never heard her complain. She had just walked out on a disastrous marriage that had lasted a little over eight years, and she was too thankful for her new-found freedom to worry about things like poverty and overwork.

Her practical attitude to life amazed me – me, who found it hard to manage my bank balance, who found the mundane chores of daily life too much of a distraction . . .

She once accused me of having it too easy, of never having to face real hardship, and I had to agree that she was right.

There were times, though, when her pragmatism did her a disservice. She often failed to appreciate the truly wondrous in life: she fought shy of my romanticism as if it were a disease. She could be cutting about my flights of fancy, my wild speculations about life on other worlds, the possibilities of the future. On these occasions she would stare at me, a frown twisting her features, and then give her head that quick irritable, bird-like shake. 'But what does all that matter!' she would say – as if all that did matter was a strict and limiting adherence to the banality of the everyday. She had gone through a lot: she was content with her present, when compared to her past. She feared, I thought, the uncertainty of the future.

We never argued about our differences, though. I loved her too much to risk creating a rift.

'Daniel,' she said, her sudden sharp tone causing me to flinch. 'You're miles away. You haven't been listening to a word . . . I might as well be talking to myself!'

'I was thinking about a dream I had last night.'

Why did I say this? I knew that she hated hearing about my dreams. She didn't dream herself, or if she did then she failed to recall them. It was as if the evidence of my over-active sleeping imagination was something that she could not understand, or therefore control.

I had dreamed of meeting a fellow writer in an ancient library filled with mouldering tomes. I had gestured around us, implying without words the insignificance of our efforts to add our slight fictions to the vast collection.

The writer had smiled, his face thin, hair gun-metal grey – a weathered and experienced face. He replied that the very act of imagining, of creating worlds that had never existed, was the true measure of our humanity.

The dream had ended there, faded from my memory even though I retained the subtle, nagging impression that our conversation had continued. Even stranger was the fact that, when I awoke, I was filled with the notion that my partner in the library had been Vaughan Edwards.

More than anything I wanted to recount my dream to Mina, but I was too wary of her scepticism. I wanted to tell her that to create worlds that had never existed was the true measure of our humanity.

· · ·

I frequently feel the need to lie about my profession. When people ask what I do, I want to answer anything but that I am a freelance writer. I am sick and tired of repeating the same old clichés in response to the same old questions. When I told Mina this, she was horrified, appalled that I should lie about what I do. Perhaps it's because Mina is so sparing with the details of her personal life that she feels the few she does divulge must be truthful, and cannot imagine anyone else thinking otherwise.

From the personal journals of Daniel Ellis.

We parked on the outskirts and walked across the Museum Street bridge and into the city centre. Even on a freezing winter Thursday the narrow streets were packed with tourists, those latter-day disciples of commerce: mainly diminutive, flat-footed Japanese with their incorrigible smiles and impeccable manners. A few large Americans provided a stark contrast. We took in one bookshop before lunch, an expensive antiquarian dealer situated along Petergate. Mina lost herself in the classics section, while I scanned the packed shelves for those forgotten fabulists of the forties, fifties and sixties, De Polnay and Wellard, Standish and Robin Maugham, minor writers who, despite infelicities, spoke to something in my soul. They were absent from the shelves of this exclusive establishment – their third-rate novels neither sufficiently ancient, nor collectable enough, to warrant stocking.

Mina bought a volume of Jane Austen's letters, I an early edition of Poe. We emerged into the ice-cold air and hurried to our favourite tea-room.

Was it a failing in me that I preferred to have Mina to myself – the jealous lover, hoarding his treasure? I could never truly appreciate her when in the company of others. I was always conscious of wanting her attention, of wanting to give her my full attention, without being observed.

One to one we would chat about nothing in particular, the people we knew in town, friends, incidents that had made the news. That day she asked me how the book was going, and I tried to keep the weariness from my tone as I recounted the novelisation's hackneyed storyline.

Early in our relationship I had told her that my writing was just another job, something I did to keep the wolf from the door. I had been writing for almost twenty-five years, and though the act of creating still struck me as edifying and worthwhile, it no longer possessed the thrill I recalled from the first five years. She had said that I must be proud of what I did, and I replied that pride was the last thing I felt.

She had looked at me with that cool, assessing gaze of hers, and said, 'Well, I'm proud of you.'

Now I ate my salad sandwich and fielded her questions about my next serious novel.

How could I tell her that, for the time being, I had shelved plans for the next book, the yearly novel that would appear under my own name? The last one had sold poorly; my editor had refused to offer an advance for another. My agent had found some hackwork to tide me over, and I had put off thinking about the next Daniel Ellis novel.

I changed the subject, asked her about her sister, Liz, and for the next fifteen minutes lost myself in contemplation of her face: square, large-eyed, attractive in that worn, mid-thirties way that signals experience with fine lines about the eyes. The face of the woman I loved.

We left the tea-room and ambled through the cobbled streets towards the Minster. She took my arm, smiling at the Christmas window displays on either hand.

Then she stopped and tugged at me. 'Daniel, look. I don't recall . . .'

It was a second-hand bookshop crammed into the interstice between a gift shop and an establishment selling a thousand types of tea. The lighted window displayed a promising selection of old first editions. Mina was already dragging me inside.

The interior of the premises opened up like an optical illusion, belying the parsimonious dimensions of its frontage. It diminished in perspective like a tunnel, and narrow wooden stairs gave access to further floors.

Mina was soon chatting to the proprietor, an owl-faced, bespectacled man in his seventies. 'We moved in just last week,' he was saying. 'Had a place beyond the Minster – too quiet. You're looking for the Victorians? You'll find them in the first room on the second floor.'

I followed her up the precipitous staircase, itself made even narrower by shelves of books on everything from angling to bee-keeping, gardening to rambling.

Mina laughed to herself on entering the well-stocked room, turned to me with the conspiratorial grin of the fellow bibliophile. While she lost herself in awed contemplation of the treasures in stock, I saw a sign above a door leading to a second room: Twentieth Century Fiction.

I stepped through, as excited as a boy given the run of a toyshop on Christmas Eve.

The room was packed from floor to ceiling with several thousand volumes. At a glance I knew that many dated from the thirties and forties: the tell-tale blanched pink spines of Hutchinson editions, the pen and ink illustrated dust-jackets so popular at the time. The room had about it an air of neglect, the junk room where musty volumes were put out to pasture before the ultimate indignity of the council skip.

I found a Robert Nathan for one pound, a Wellard I did not possess for £1.50. I remembered Vaughan Edwards, and moved with anticipation to the E section. There were plenty of Es, but no Edwards.

I moved on, disappointed, but still excited by the possibility of more treasures to be found. I was scanning the shelves for Rupert Croft-Cooke when Mina called out from the next room, 'Daniel. Here.'

She had a stack of thick volumes piled beside her on the bare floorboards, and was holding out a book to me. 'Look.'

I expected some title she had been looking out for, but the book was certainly not Victorian. It had the modern, maroon boards of something published in the fifties.

'Isn't he the writer you mentioned the other week?'

I read the spine. *A Bitter Recollection* – Vaughan Edwards.

I opened the book, taking in the publishing details, the full-masted galleon symbol of the publisher, Longmans, Green and Company. It was his fourth novel, published in 1958.

I read the opening paragraph, and something clicked. I knew I had stumbled across a like soul.

An overnight frost had sealed the ploughed fields like so much stiffened corduroy, and in the distance, mist shrouded and remote, stood the village of Low Dearing. William Barnes, stepping from the second-class carriage onto the empty platform, knew at once that this was the place.

'Where did you find it?' I asked, hoping that there might be others by the author.

She laughed. 'Where do you think? Where it belongs, on the 50p shelf.'

She indicated a free-standing bookcase crammed with a miscellaneous selection of oddments, warped hardbacks, torn paperbacks, pamphlets and knitting patterns. There were no other books by Vaughan Edwards.

I laid my books upon her pile on the floor and took Mina in my arms. She stiffened, looking around to ensure we were quite alone: for whatever reasons, she found it difficult to show affection when we might be observed.

We made our way carefully down the stairs and

paid for our purchases. I indicated the Edwards and asked the proprietor if he had any others by the same author.

He took the book and squinted at the spine. 'Sorry, but if you'd like to leave your name and address . . .'

I did so, knowing that it would come to nothing.

We left the shop and walked back to the car, hand in hand. We drove back through the rapidly falling winter twilight, the traffic sparse on the already frost-scintillating B-roads. The gritters would be out tonight, and the thought of the cold spell gripping the land filled me with gratitude that soon I would be home, before the fire, with my purchases.

For no apparent reason, Mina laid a hand on my leg as I drove, and closed her eyes.

I appreciated her spontaneous displays of affection all the more because they were so rare and arbitrary. Sometimes the touch of her hand in mine, when she had taken it without being prompted, was like a jolt of electricity.

The moon was full, shedding a magnesium light across the fields around the cottage. As I was about to turn into the drive, the thrilling, bush-tailed shape of a fox slid across the metalled road before the car, stopped briefly to stare into the headlights, then flowed off again and disappeared into the hedge.

. . .

Through focusing minutely on the inner lives of his characters, Vaughan Edwards manages to create stories of profound honesty and humanity . . .

> From D. L. Shackleton's review of *The Tall Ghost and other stories* by Vaughan Edwards.

I began *A Bitter Recollection* that night after dinner, and finished it in the early hours, emerging from the novel with surprise that so many hours had passed. It was the first time in years that I had finished a novel in one sitting, and I closed the book with a kind of breathless exultation. It was not the finest book I had ever read – the prose was too fastidious in places, and the plotting left much to be desired – but it was one of the most emotionally honest pieces of fiction I had ever come across. It swept me up and carried me along with its tortured portrayal of the central character, William Barnes, and his quest to find his missing lover. There was a magical quality to the book, an elegiac yearning for halcyon days, a time when things were better – and at the same time the novel was informed with the tragic awareness that all such desire is illusory. Barnes never found his lover – I suspected that he was an unreliable narrator, and that Isabella never really existed, was merely an extended metaphor for that harrowing sense of loss we all carry with us without really knowing why.

I was moved to tears by the novel, and wanted more.

I wrote to a dozen second-hand bookshops up and down the country, and logged onto the Websites of book-finders on the Internet, requesting the eleven novels I had yet to read, and his two collections.

Mina read the book, at my request. I was eager for her opinion, would even watch her while she read the novel, trying to gauge how she was enjoying it. She finished the book in three days, shrugged when I asked her what she thought of it, and said, 'It lacked something.'

I stared at her. 'Is that all? What do you mean? What did it lack?'

She frowned, pulled me onto the sofa and stroked my hair, her eyes a million miles away. 'I don't know . . . I mean, it had no story. Nothing happened. It lacked drama.'

'The drama was internalised in Barnes,' I began.

'Perhaps that was the problem. I couldn't identify with him. I couldn't even feel sympathy for him and his search for Isabella.'

'I don't think Isabella existed,' I said.

She blinked at me. 'She didn't?'

'She might have been a metaphor for loss.'

Mina shook her head, exasperated. 'No wonder I couldn't engage with the thing,' she said. 'If Isabella didn't exist, then it was even emptier than I first thought. It was about nothing . . .'

'Nothing but loss,' I said.

She smiled at me. 'You liked it, didn't you?'

'I loved it.'

She shook her head, as if in wonder. 'Sometimes, Daniel, I want to see inside your head, try to understand what you're thinking, but sometimes that frightens me.'

. . .

Today I met a wonderful woman, Mina Pratt. 'I wasn't born a Pratt,' she told me, 'I just married one.' She is 36, divorced, has two children. We met in the Fleece and talked for an hour about nothing but the novels we were reading. I was instantly attracted to her. She's practical, down-to-earth, level-headed – all the things I'm not. I told her I was a writer, and cursed myself in case she thought I was trying to impress her.

From the personal journals of Daniel Ellis.

Christmas came and went.

It was Mina's turn to have the girls for that year's festivities. Her parents came over from Leeds and the house was full, for the first time in ages, with goodwill and glad tidings. I disliked Christmas – the occasion struck me as tawdry and cheap, an excuse to party when no excuse was really needed, a time of sanctimonious bonhomie towards our fellow man, and the rest of the year be damned. I withheld my humbug from Mina. She loved Christmas day, the glitz and the cosiness, the present giving . . . It was a paradox, I know. She, the hard-hearted pragmatist, and me the romantic. I could take the romantic ideal of Yule, but not the actuality, while Mina enjoyed the occasion quite simply for what it was, a chance for the family to get together, enjoy good food and a classic film on TV.

The period following Christmas, and the even sadder occasion of New Year, strikes me as the nadir of the year. Spring is a distant promise, winter a grey, bitter cold reality: if the calendar were to be rendered as an abstract visualisation, then January and February would be coloured black.

The new year was brightened, on the second Saturday of January, by the unexpected arrival of a brown cardboard package. Mina was on an early shift, and the girls – Sam and Tessa, eight and six respectively – were filling in a colouring book at the kitchen table. I tended to keep in the background on the days when Mina had the girls; even after a year, and even though it was my house, I felt as though I were trespassing on emotional territory not rightfully mine. On the rare occasions when I was alone with the girls, I would give them pens and paper, or put a video on TV, and leave them to their own devices.

I carried the package to my study at the top of the house, attempting to divine from the postmark some idea of its content. The package came from York.

Intrigued, still not guessing, I ripped it open.

Books, and books, moreover, by Vaughan Edwards: his first and third novels, *Winter at the Castle* and *A Brighter Light*. They were in good condition, complete

18
· ·

with pristine dust jackets. They looked as though they had never been read, though the passage of years had discoloured the pages to a sepia hue, and foxed the end-papers. A bargain at five pounds each, including postage and packing.

The back flap of the jackets each gave the same brief, potted biography: Vaughan Edwards was born in Dorset in 1930. After National Service in the RAF, he taught for five years at a public school in Gloucestershire. He is now a full-time writer and lives in the North Yorkshire village of Highdale.

These terse contractions of an individual's life filled me with sadness, especially those from years ago. I always read them in the knowledge that the life described was now no more, or was at least much altered in circumstance. I thought of Vaughan Edwards in the RAF, then teaching, and then living the writer's life in Highdale . . . before the tragedy of his disappearance.

Highdale was a small village situated thirty miles from Skipton on the North Yorkshire moors. It occurred to me that Edwards might still have been living there at the time of his disappearance, six years ago.

I rationed myself, over the course of the following bitter cold days, to just three hours a night with the novels of Vaughan Edwards. While Mina curled in her chair and reread the Brontës, I lay on the sofa and slowly immersed myself in the singular world of the vanished novelist. I began with his first novel, *Winter at the Castle*, a strange story of a group of lonely and embittered individuals who find themselves invited for a month to the remote Northumbrian castle of a reclusive landowner. That the recluse never appears to the guests, nor in the novel, came as no surprise. There was no explanation as to why they might have been invited to the castle. There was little action, but much introspection, as the characters met, interacted, and discussed their respective lives – and then left to resume their places in a century that hardly suited them . . . I refrained from asking Mina what she might make of this one.

His third novel, *A Brighter Light*, was a monologue from the viewpoint of a young girl imprisoned in an oak tree, her recollections of her early life, and how her essence had become one with the oak. She befriended, through a form of telepathy, a young novelist who moved into the cottage where the tree grew. The book ends ambiguously; there is a hint that the man joins the girl's spirit in the tree, and also that the monologue might have been a fictional work by the young writer.

Unpromising subject matter, I had to admit that. In the hands of a lesser writer, the novels would just not work. But something in Vaughan Edwards' mature handling of his characters' emotions, their honestly wrought inner lives, lifted the books from the level of turgid emotionalism and invested them with art.

I finished *A Brighter Light* and laid it aside, my heart hammering.

Mina smiled across at me. 'Good?'

'Amazing.'

'I'll believe you,' she laughed.

Like all great art, which I believed these books to be, they had the effect of making me look anew at my life and the world around me; it was as if I saw Mina for the first time, was able now, with perceptions honed by 'Edwards' insight, to discern her essence, the bright light that burned at the core of her being. I felt then an overwhelming surge of love for this woman, and at the same time I was cut through with sadness like a physical pain.

Early in our relationship, she had told me that she did not love me, and that, 'I can't bring myself to feel love for anyone, other than the girls.'

I accepted this, rationalised that perhaps in time she might come to appreciate me, might even one day bring herself to love me.

I had asked her if she was unable to feel love because she had invested so much in her husband, only for that investment to turn sour. Perhaps she was afraid, I suggested, to risk giving love again, for fear of being hurt a second time. She denied this, said that she could not explain her inability to love me. I told myself that she was either deluding herself, or lying. Perhaps she was lying to save my feelings; perhaps she was capable of love, but I was not the right person. In the early days I was torn by the pain of what I saw as rejection . . . and yet she remained with me, gave a passable impression of, if not love, then a deep affection, and I refrained from quizzing her as to the state of her heart, and learned to live from day to day.

'Mina,' I said now. 'I love you.'

She sighed and closed her eyes, and then snapped them open and stared at me. 'Daniel, I wish you wouldn't . . .' Her plea was heartfelt.

'Sorry. Had to tell you. Sorry if that disturbs you. You know, most women like to be told that they're loved.'

'Well, I'm not most women—'

'I'm not going to leave you, Mina. You can tell me that you love me, and I won't walk out, hurt you again—'

'Oh, Christ!' She sat up and stared across at me. 'Why do you have to analyse? Why now? Everything's been fine, hasn't it? I'm here, with you. What more do you want?'

What more did I want?

Perhaps it was possessive of me to demand her love when I had everything else she could give me? Perhaps she was simply being honest when she admitted that she could not extend to me something that she claimed she no longer believed in. Perhaps I was an insecure, thoughtless bastard for demanding that she should open her heart.

'I'm sorry. I just wanted you to know.'

She sat and stared at me, as if at a wounded animal. In a small voice she said, 'I know, Daniel. I know.'

. . .

Mina's professed inability to feel love for me can only be a reaction to what she went through with her husband. She denies this – but is this denial her way of not admitting me past her defences, of not allowing me a glimpse of her true feelings and emotions?

> From the personal journals of Daniel Ellis.

The following week I received an e-mail from a second-hand bookshop in Oxford, informing me that they had located three novels by Vaughan Edwards. I sent a cheque and the books arrived a few days later.

One of the novels was his very last, *The Secret of Rising Dene*, published shortly after his disappearance. The biographical details made no reference to the fact that he had vanished, but did give the interesting information that, in '96, he was still living in the North Yorkshire village of Highdale.

That weekend I suggested a drive up into the Dales. I told Mina that I wanted to visit Highdale, where Edwards had lived. After the spat the previous week, things had been fine between us. She made no mention of my interrogative *faux pas*, and I did my best not to rile her with further questions.

'Highdale? Don't we go through Settle to get there? There's that wonderful Thai place on the way.'

'Okay, we'll call in on the way back. How's that?'

She laughed at me. 'I hope you don't expect Highdale to be a shrine to your literary hero,' she said. 'He wasn't quite in the same league as the Brontës—'

'Then let's hope that Highdale isn't as trashily commercialised as Haworth, okay?'

Deuce.

She elbowed me in the ribs.

TWO

We set off after lunch on an unusually bright February afternoon, dazzling sunlight giving the false promise of the spring to come – which would soon no doubt be dashed by the next bout of bitter cold and rain.

The approach road to the village of Highdale wound through ancient woodland on the side of a steep hill. When we reached the crest I pulled off the road and braked the car.

I laughed in delight. The sunlight picked out the village with great golden searchlights falling through low banks of cumulus. Highdale was a collection of tiny stone-built cottages and farmhouses set amid hunched pastures; I made out a church, a public house, and what might have been a village hall, all laid out below us like some sanguine architect's scale model of a rural idyll.

We drove down the incline and into the village and parked on the cobbled market square before the White Lion.

The pub was empty, save for a barman chatting to

someone who might have been a local farmer. They both looked up when we pushed through the door, as if unaccustomed to customers at this time of day.

I ordered a dry cider for Mina and a fresh orange juice for myself. While the barman poured the drinks and chatted to Mina, I looked around the snug. It was fitted out much like any typical village pub: a variety of moorland scenes by local artists, a selection of horse brasses, a battalion of Toby jugs hanging in ranks from the low, blackened beams.

Then I noticed the bookshelf, or rather the books that were upon it. One volume in particular stood out – I recognised the Val Biro pen and ink sketch on the spine of the dust jacket. It showed the attenuated figure of a man doffing his Trilby. It was the cover of Vaughan Edwards' third novel, *A Brighter Light*.

The barman said something.

'Excuse me?' I said, my attention on the books.

'I think he wants paying,' Mina said. 'Don't worry, I'll get these.'

She paid the barman and carried the drinks over to the table beneath the bookshelf. I was peering at the racked spines, head tilted.

'Good God,' I said. 'They're all Edwards.'

'Not all of them.' Mina tapped the spines of four books, older volumes than the Edwards. They were by a writer I had never come across before, E.V. Cunningham-Price. They looked Victorian, and caught her interest. She pulled them from the shelf, sat down and began reading.

I sorted through the Edwards. There were ten novels, eight of which I had never read, and a volume of short stories. I pulled them down and stacked them on the table, reading through the description of each book on the front inside flap.

I looked back at the shelf. I thought it odd that there should be no other books beside the Edwards and the four Cunningham-Price volumes.

The barman was watching me. I hefted one of the books. 'They're not for sale, by any chance . . . ?'

He was a big man in his sixties, with the type of stolid, typically northern face upon which scowls seem natural, like fissures in sedimentary rock.

'Well, by rights they're not for sale, like. They're for the enjoyment of the customers, if you know what I mean. Tell you what, though – take a couple with you, if you promise to bring them back.'

'I'll do that. That's kind—'

'You're not locals, then?'

Mina looked up. 'Almost. Skipton.'

'Local enough,' the barman said. 'Hope you enjoy 'em.'

'I'm sure I will.' I paused, regarding the books and wondering which two volumes to take with me. Mina looked up from her book. 'I wouldn't mind taking this one, Daniel.'

I selected the volume of stories, *The Tall Ghost and other stories*, and returned the others to the shelf.

I finished my drink and moved to the bar for a refill. I indicated the books. 'He was a local, wasn't he? Did he ever drop by?'

'Mr Vaughan?' the barman asked. 'Every Monday evening, regular as clockwork. Sat on the stool over there.' He indicated a high stool placed by the corner of the bar and the wall. 'Drank three Irish whiskeys from nine until ten, then left on the dot of the hour. Very rarely missed a Monday for over twenty years.'

'You knew him well?'

'Mr Vaughan?' He grunted a humourless laugh. 'No one knew Mr Vaughan. Kept himself to himself, if you know what I mean. Spoke to no one, and no one spoke to him. Reckon that's how he preferred it. Lived here nigh on forty years, and never said boo to a goose.'

'Strange,' I said, sipping my juice.

'Well,' the publican said, 'he was a writer chappie, you know?' He tapped his head. 'Lived up here most of the time.'

Over at her table, Mina was smiling to herself.

'He had a place in the village?' I asked.

'Not far off. He owned the big house up the hill on your left as you come in, set back in the woods. Edge-coombe Hall.'

The very title fired my imagination. It seemed somehow fitting, the very place where Vaughan Edwards would have lived his sequestered, writer's life.

I decided I'd like to take a look at the place. 'Who owns it now?'

'Edgecoombe Hall?' He shook his head. 'No one. It's been standing empty ever since Mr Vaughan went and disappeared.'

I nodded, digesting this. If it were a big house, with a fair bit of land, and perhaps dilapidated, then I imagined that no local would care to touch the place, and High-dale was just too far off the beaten track to make commuting to Leeds or Bradford an option for a pro-spective city buyer.

'Why's that?' I asked.

The publican shrugged. 'Well, it's not exactly brand spanking new,' he said. 'A bit tumbledown, if you know what I mean. And the ghost doesn't help.'

At this, Mina looked up from her book. 'The ghost?' She had scepticism daubed across her face in primary colours. She gave me a look that said, *if you believe that, Daniel* . . .

'Only reporting what I was told, love. Don't believe in 'em meself. Old wives' tales.'

Despite myself, I was intrigued. 'The ghost of Vaughan Edwards, right?'

He shook his head. Behind me, I heard Mina sigh with mock despair. 'That's where you're wrong, sir. The Hall was haunted – if you believe in that kind of thing –

long before Mr Vaughan bought the place. Stories go way back, right to the turn of the century – and I mean the century before last. 1900s. Ghost of a young girl haunts the place every full moon, so they say. Many a local claims to have clapped eyes on it.'

I drank my orange juice and considered Vaughan Edwards. The scant biographical information I had come across had never mentioned whether or not he had ever married.

I asked the publican.

'Married? Mr Vaughan?' He chuckled. 'Never saw him with a woman – nor anyone else, for that matter. Bit of a recluse.'

'So he lived alone in the Hall?'

The publican laughed. 'Alone, if you don't count the ghost.'

I noticed that Mina had finished her drink and was gesturing to go. I signalled one minute and turned to my informant. 'You don't happen to know anything about how he disappeared?'

Mina sighed.

The publican said, 'Strange do, all things considered. His car was found in the woods, not a hundred yards up from the Hall, on the track leading to the escarpment above the river. A local youth found it and notified the police. They investigated, found he wasn't at the Hall, then traced his footprints on the path leading to the drop.' He shrugged. 'Strange thing was, his footprints stopped before they reached the edge.' He paused, considering. ''Course, he could always have stepped off the path and walked to the edge through the bracken.'

'You think that's what he did? Threw himself off the escarpment into the river?'

'Me?' He gave my question due consideration. 'I don't rightly know, sir. He didn't seem the kind to do a thing like that, but then who can tell? You see, his body was never found, which struck me as strange. The river's fast flowing, but there's a mill dam about two miles south of here. The body would've fetched up there, all things considered.'

'So if he didn't kill himself,' I asked, 'then what happened?'

'Aha,' the publican said, 'now that's the sixty-four thousand dollar question, isn't it?'

He paused, watching me. 'Funny thing, though,' he went on.

'Yes?'

'About a week before he disappeared, he brought in this carrier bag full of books. A dozen or so of his own and four or five others by the Cunningham chappie. He just dropped the bag on the counter and said that the far shelf needed filling, and that was it. Not another word.'

I nodded. 'Strange.'

We were interrupted by the arrival of another customer. 'Usual, Bill?' the publican called, and moved down the bar to pull a pint of Tetley's.

Mina took the opportunity to hurry me from the place. I picked up the Edwards collection, thanked the landlord and followed Mina outside.

As we drove up the hill and out of the village, she said, 'You really believed all that rubbish, didn't you?'

I glanced at her. 'What rubbish?'

'All that about the ghost.'

'I don't believe it – but then again I don't necessarily disbelieve.'

She said, 'I don't know . . .' under her breath.

'What's wrong with keeping your options open, Mina? "There are more things in heaven and earth, Horatio . . ." Look at it this way, how many things were dismissed as impossible a hundred years ago, which have come to be accepted now?'

'Ghosts aren't one of them,' she said.

I sighed. I often found her world view severely limiting, and it irritated me when she took to mocking my open-mindedness.

I wondered if she had always been a sceptic, or if having to concentrate wholly on the practicalities of day to day survival during the traumatic separation from her husband had fostered in her such a narrow perspective. She would give credence to nothing that she could not see before her, that she could not grasp.

I drove slowly up the hillside, looking through the trees for sign of Edgecoombe Hall.

'Couldn't you see that he was leading you on, Daniel?' she continued.

'The publican?'

'He was spinning a yarn. I wonder how many times he's told the same story to visitors?'

I shook my head. 'I don't think so. He said himself that he didn't believe in ghosts.'

'And that story of Edwards' disappearance—'

I turned to her, wide-eyed. 'Don't tell me, Mina – you refuse to believe in that, too?'

She struck my arm with playful truculence. 'He was going on as if he might have survived – I don't know, staged his own disappearance. The chances are he left his car and went for a walk, went too near the edge and fell into the river.'

'So why was his body never discovered?'

She shrugged. 'Search me. Maybe it got snagged on the river-bottom.'

'Surely it would've been discovered by now.'

'So what do you think happened then?'

I smiled to myself. She loved certainty. I shook my head. 'I just don't know,' I said, knowing it would exasperate her. 'Ah . . . Look.'

I braked and pulled into the side of the road. Through the winter-denuded sycamore and elm, set perhaps half a mile from the road, I made out the gaunt towers of a Victorian building.

'Edgecoombe Hall, I presume. Mind if we take a look?'

She surprised me. She was staring at the severe outline of the Hall, something speculative in her gaze. 'Why not?' she said at last.

I drove on a little further, looking for the opening to the driveway in the overgrown hedge of ivy and bramble.

'There,' she called, pointing to a gap in the hedge. Once, many years ago, two tall stone pillars, topped with orbs, had marked the entrance to the grounds; now the pillars were cloaked with ivy. Wrought iron gates hung open and awry, their hinges having rusted long ago.

I turned the car into the pot-holed driveway and proceeded at walking pace through the gloomy tunnel between overgrown rhododendron and elderberry bushes.

Edgecoombe Hall hove into sight, more stark and intimidating at close quarters than when seen from the road. It was a foursquare pile with mock-Gothic towers at each corner, its façade having long ago given up the ghost against the creeping tide of ivy. Only the double doorway and a couple of upstairs windows were free of the verdant mass.

It struck me as the appropriate domicile of a lonely and reclusive writer. I almost expected to see a massive, haunted oak tree in the middle of the lawn, or the ghostly face of a young girl peering timidly out through an upper window.

I stopped the car before the plinth of steps rising to the entrance. Mina laid a hand on my arm and pointed.

A small truck, laden with timber, was parked around the far corner of the Hall. 'Perhaps someone has bought it after all,' she said. She peered at the façade and pulled a face. 'Certainly needs work.'

We climbed out. The sun was setting through the trees, slanting an intense orange light across the lawn and illuminating the ivied frontage of the building. I moved away from the car, stood and took in the atmosphere of the place.

Far from intimidating, the Hall seemed to me a place of melancholy. Perhaps it was merely that it was in a state of such disrepair, had seen far, far better days. But I imagined the Hall as it might have been, shorn of ivy and pristine, and it came to me still that it would have been a dour and eldritch place.

A steady tattoo of hammer blows sounded from within the Hall, and it cheered me that someone was at least making a start at renovation.

'Daniel,' Mina said. 'Look.'

She was pointing at the ground, the gravelled drive that swept around the front of the building. I joined her.

A series of fissures radiated from the Hall, wide where they issued from the wall and narrowing as they crossed the drive. I noticed great cracks in the grey brickwork beneath the ivy.

'Looks like it's been hit by an earthquake,' she said.

I approached the façade, where I guessed a window might be positioned behind the ivy, and pulled away the clinging growth. I came to a mullioned pane and peered within. A bright spear of sunlight fell over my shoulder and illuminated the room. To my surprise it was furnished: bookshelves lined the walls, and elephantine armchairs and sofas were positioned before the hearth.

'See anything?'

I held a swatch of vine aside as she peered in. She shivered theatrically. 'Creepy.'

I was about to suggest that we enter the Hall and find the wielder of the hammer, but Mina had other ideas. She took my arm. 'You've seen enough, Daniel. I'm hungry. A Thai banquet awaits us.'

The thought of food appealed to me, too. I wanted to stay a little longer, but I also wanted to investigate the track which Vaughan Edwards had taken prior to his disappearance.

'Okay, but there's something I must check, first.'

Mina rolled her eyes. I took her arm and we returned to the car. 'What?' she asked.

I reversed, then drove down the drive and onto the road. I turned right, continuing up the hill, and kept a lookout for a track leading into the woods.

I found it, and turned. Twilight enclosed us. 'Daniel,' Mina warned me.

'This, if I'm not mistaken, is where Vaughan Edwards left his car on the day he disappeared.'

Ahead of us the track terminated in a clearing made magical by the dying light of the sun. When I cut the engine and opened the door, a deathly hush pervaded the clearing and I received the distinct impression that the place regarded our arrival as an intrusion.

I climbed out and stood beside the car. In the gathering dusk I made out a worn path leading through the trees. I gestured for Mina to join me. She sat in the passenger seat, frowning her displeasure, waited a beat and then flounced out with ill grace.

'All I can think about is green Thai curry and you want to drag me through the mud on a wild goose chase.' As is often the case with Mina, the tone of her voice was betrayed by the humorous light of tolerance in her eyes.

She took my hand and we hurried side by side along the footpath.

Perhaps it was the writer in me, the pathological creator of tales, but I was storing away this setting, and the feelings I was experiencing, for use in some future work of fiction. I was filled with the sense that time had dissolved, that all events maintained simultaneously, and that any second I might behold the figure of Vaughan Edwards striding towards his destiny through the undergrowth before us.

The path took a sharp turn to the left, and the trees

thinned out: an aqueous, twilight lacuna glimmered before us.

'Stop!' Mina screamed, clutching my arm.

I halted, stock still. At my feet the earth crumbled away, and only then did I make out the sudden drop.

Mina hauled me back and we stood, our arms about each other like frightened children, and stared in wonder and fright at the suddenly revealed precipice.

Emboldened by survival, I took a step forward and made out, a hundred feet below, the muscled torrent of a river in full spate.

I rejoined Mina. She was staring at me.

'Perhaps that's what happened to your writer,' she whispered, staring down.

'And his body?'

She shrugged, then gave a little shiver. 'I don't know.' She paused, as if considering. 'Let's go, Daniel. I don't like it here.'

'I thought you didn't believe in ghosts,' I said.

She snorted. 'I believe in the power of auto-suggestion,' she replied.

We retraced our way back along the path to the clearing. I was heartened to see the car – as if some primitive part of me had feared that it might have vanished in our absence, stranding us in the haunted wood. I kept my musings to myself as I backed from the clearing and once again resumed the road, heading for Settle.

Over piled plates of green curry and five-mushroom satay, we chatted. Mina was animated and affectionate, as if she wished to put from her mind all thought of Vaughan Edwards and Edgecoombe Hall, and concentrate instead on the simple commerce of intimacy. She laughed a lot, reached across the table to touch my hand – an uncommon gesture – and got a little tipsy on Singha beer.

I'd often lose myself in the miracle of her physicality, staring into her wide eyes, or at her exquisite hands. Mina had the finest hands I had ever seen; small, ineffably graceful, with a lithe, articulated elegance and long, oval nails. And these were hands that made a dozen beds a day, that mopped up after incontinent patients, washed and cooked and cared for two children and myself . . .

Ten months ago her hours at the hospital had been cut and the rent of her terraced house increased, and for two weeks she had fretted without telling me of her concern. When at last I asked her what was wrong, and she told me, I rashly escalated the terms of our relationship by suggesting that she move in with me. Until then she had always stipulated that I stay over at her place only twice a week, that she was not committed to me – and I had feared that my offer might frighten her away.

To my joy she had agreed, and moved in, and I had adapted myself to part-time family life, careful not to impose myself on Mina in any way, to maintain a

distance with the girls, not wanting to be seen to be
usurping her maternal authority. For months I had
walked on egg-shells.

I had never asked her if, even without the financial
necessity, she would have eventually moved in with
me. She hated my analysis of our relationship, the
stripping to basics of her motivations. From time to
time it came to me that she was with me not through
bonds of strong affection, but merely because I was, to
put it crudely, a meal ticket.

On these occasions I told myself that I should be
thankful that I had found someone whom I could love,
and left it at that.

We finished the meal and drove home through a
frosty, star-filled night. It was as if we had agreed tacitly
not to mention Edwards and the Hall. Mina laid a hand
on my leg and talked of work, but I was conscious of the
weight of the book in my jacket pocket, waiting to be
read, at once inviting and, for some reason I could not
quite fathom, not a little threatening.

· · ·

'Vaughan Edwards manages to capture the tragic truth of
the human condition in his timeless works of fiction . . .'
Graham Greene, cover quote for *A Summer's Promise*.

One month passed.

For some reason, I could not bring myself to read the
Vaughan Edwards collection of stories I had borrowed

from the White Lion. The book remained on my desk, unopened. From time to time I would pick it up, admire the Val Biro cover of a village scene with a Maypole as the centre-piece, and read the description of the stories on the inside flap, and the scant biographical paragraph on the back. But I felt a strange reluctance to begin the book.

I wondered if, subconsciously, I identified Vaughan Edwards and his books with Mina's uneasiness at Edgecoombe Hall that day. That weak core of my being, insecure in our relationship, was eager to appease Mina in whichever way possible – even if that meant not reading *The Tall Ghost and other stories*.

How Mina would have laughed at my tortured self-analysis!

However, as the weeks since Edgecoombe Hall elapsed, our relationship seemed to take on a new dimension, become deeper and more fulfilling. Mina did not go so far as to profess her undying love for me, but she did become more affectionate. Our love-making – never breathlessly passionate – increased in regularity and scope: it seemed that suddenly we each learned more of the other's desires, and adapted accordingly. As ever, these things went unspoken between us. Mina was a great believer that things should happen of their own accord, intuitively, an attitude which I – forever needing to question and analyse – found maddening. I bit my tongue, however. The last thing I wanted was to anger her by asking how she thought our relationship might be progressing.

A month after Edgecoombe Hall, it came to me that my reluctance to read the collection was nothing more than groundless insecurity. I looked back at my self-censorship and something in me, forever critical of my behaviour, mocked such feeble-mindedness.

I began the book when Mina was working a night-shift. While a wind keened around the cottage, rattling the windows in their frames, I lay on the sofa and immersed myself in Vaughan Edwards' singular visions.

The stories, written in the late forties and fifties and first published in magazines as diverse as *Lilliput* and the American *Magazine of Fantasy and Science Fiction*, were, if anything, even stranger than his novels. They comprised routine ghost stories, eerie fantasy tales set in the far future and the distant past, and two tales quite unclassifiable. These stories I found the most compelling. They told of visitors to Earth – though from where they came was never disclosed – their relations with lonely human beings, their perceptions of each other, and their attempts at conveying a sense of their separate realities. The impossibility of ever wholly comprehending an alien's viewpoint made for frustrating, if occasionally intriguing, reading. I finished the book in the early hours of the morning, convinced that I had been granted a privileged glimpse into the brilliant, if tortured, psyche of a fellow human being.

That morning we remained in bed until eleven, made love, and then lay in each other's arms. The harsh summons of the telephone propelled Mina to her feet. I watched her stalk around the bed and retrieve her dressing-gown from the back of the door. Short and heavy-breasted, she reminded me of the earth-goddess figurines of the Palaeolithic period, full-bodied idols of fertility.

While she spoke on the phone – it was her sister, arranging a drink for that night – I stared at the ceiling and wondered whether to tell her that I was planning another trip to Highdale. I would return the two books we had borrowed, and ask if I could take the remaining Edwards if I left a monetary deposit.

Mina came back, shed her dressing-gown and slipped into bed beside me, gloriously naked. She slung a leg over my hip and told me that she was seeing Liz that night at the Fleece.

She met her sister perhaps once a week for a customary four halves of cider, and each time she left the house I could not help but experience an involuntary and wholly unwarranted pang of jealousy. Mina lived up to the archetype of a nurse in her extrovert ability to engage socially with all and everybody; men found her not only physically attractive, but open and approachable. She was popular, and outgoing, and the immature child in me, like a boy who demands his mother's total attention, bridled at the fact of her sociability.

Of course, I hated myself for this . . . And, of course, I had never mentioned it to Mina.

She had once, months ago, told me that she could never feel jealous. When I expressed disbelief, she quoted an instance. When she was leaving her husband he, in a bid to make her jealous and win her back, made it obvious that he was seeing another woman. She said she had felt nothing, other than relief that it made her decision to leave him all the more clear cut.

I refrained from pointing out to her that of course she would not feel jealous of someone who, by that point, she had come to hate.

Now I held her to me and let slip, quite casually, that the following day I intended to drive up to Highdale.

She pulled away to get a better look at me. 'You're not going to look around that house again, are you?'

I shook my head. 'I want to collect the remaining Edwards books I haven't read.'

'You can only take two at a time, remember?'

I laughed. 'It isn't a lending library. I'll leave him a deposit and take the lot.'

She regarded me. 'You really like his stuff, don't you?'

'It's magical.'

'I don't like it, Daniel. There's something . . . I don't know, not exactly creepy . . .' She stopped and stared at the ceiling. 'There's some quality about his books that frightens me. Perhaps it's just that I like certainty. I like to know that everything has its place. With his stories, his reality is off-centre, skewed.' She shivered. 'Enough of Vaughan Edwards. Aren't you getting up today?'

'Not working.' I yawned.

'No?' She looked at me, concerned. 'You haven't worked for weeks.'

Getting on for two months, to be precise. The creative urge had left me, and I had no pressing financial need to commit another novelisation. A week earlier my agent had phoned, asking how the latest novel was shaping up. He said that, despite the fact that my publisher might be wary of looking at the next one, he was sure he could interest a senior editor at HarperCollins.

I had lied – the fantasy springing easily to my lips – that it was going okay, was still in the early stages; that, as he knew, I didn't like to talk about work in progress. I had replaced the receiver with a nagging sense of shame at the lie.

'When there's no bread on the table, Mina, then we'll worry, okay?'

She looked at me. 'I'll make breakfast, Daniel.'

As I lay in bed and listened to the blissful sound of domesticity going on in the kitchen, the sizzling of eggs, the perking of the coffee, I wondered about the next book, and my lack of desire to start it. Never before had I been pole-axed by such apathy, even in my twenties when I had written novel after bad novel with no hope of finding a publisher.

I told myself that the muse would return, one day, and went downstairs to join Mina for breakfast.

· · ·

'I don't give a damn about things like facts in my novels. My books aren't about the factual, physical world. They're about what's in here. Critics may call my work old-fashioned and over-emotional, but I contend that our emotions are the only true barometer of our humanity.'

Vaughan Edwards, in a rare radio interview,
BBC Third Programme, April 1959.

That afternoon, when I emerged from my study after doodling for a futile hour over the rewrite of a short story, Mina was kneeling on the rug before the fire, rump in the air. She had three books open on the floor, and was looking from one to the other, lost in concentration.

The girls were home from school, watching a noisy video on the TV in the kitchen.

Mina saw me and blinked, her face quite blank.

'What's wrong?' I asked.

I saw that the books she was studying were the E.V. Cunningham-Price and two of Vaughan Edwards' novels.

I moved to the kitchen and closed the door, diminishing the cartoon din.

'Daniel . . . This is strange.'

'What's strange?' Oddly enough, and for no apparent reason, I was aware of my increased pulse.

She stabbed at a book with a graceful forefinger. I sat on the sofa, watching her.

'This. I was reading the Cunningham-Price. There's a chapter set in North Yorkshire, about an artist who lives alone in a big house. It's haunted, and the artist has an affair with the ghost of a young girl . . .'

My stomach turned.

Mina went on, 'I remember you telling me about Edwards' book, *The Miracle at Hazelmere*. It sounded pretty much the same, so I checked. And look.'

She passed me the Cunningham-Price and *Miracle*. Disbelieving, and feeling a little strange, I read passages from both books that she had marked with yellow Post-it notes. For the next hour I went through the books, while Mina prepared the girls for ballet lessons. She looked in on me before setting off. 'What do you think?'

I looked up, nodded. 'Remarkable. He must have used the Cunningham book as a template . . .'

'You mean he plagiarised,' she said. 'I'll be back in an hour.'

I nodded again, absently. 'I'll have dinner ready.'

'That'd be great.' She hurried from the room. The video noise ceased, and suddenly the cottage was deathly quiet.

I read through the Cunningham-Price book, discovering many thematic similarities between it and other of Edwards' novels. My first fear, that Edwards had merely lifted great chunks of Cunningham-Price and claimed them as his own, was not borne out. Although, as Mina had rightly pointed out, Edwards had used an episode in the Cunningham-Price and expanded it, delving into the themes and ideas that Cunningham-Price had left unexplored, I was loath to accuse the modern novelist of plagiarising the Victorian. Rather, it was as if he had read the Cunningham-Price, found himself fascinated with the Victorian's ideas and concepts, and fleshed them out in his own fiction: Edwards' work, far from plagiarism, struck me as a tribute – acknowledged when he used certain of the older writer's characters and situations. A simple plagiarist without talent would simply have copied, not used Cunningham-Price as a starting point from which to explore his own ideas.

I recalled my promise to prepare dinner, and moved to the kitchen.

Later that night, with the girls in bed, I served dinner and opened a bottle of wine, and we discussed Mina's literary discovery.

'Think it'll earn me a footnote in some encyclopaedia?' she asked.

'More like a whole damn entry.'

She sipped her wine. 'But why would he do it, Daniel? Why would a writer simply steal another writer's work?'

I pointed my fork at her. 'I don't think he did,' I said. I explained my theory that Edwards had used

Cunningham-Price as a starting point, and as a matter of course had acknowledged the Victorian writer by echoing some of his events and characters.

Mina stared at me. 'Echoing?' she laughed. 'That's the strangest euphemism for plagiarism I've ever heard.'

'Mina, Edwards is no plagiarist. He's too talented for that.'

'You just don't want to admit that your literary hero is a word-burglar, Daniel!'

I smiled at her turn of phrase. 'There's one way to find out for sure. Tomorrow I'll go up to Highdale and fetch the rest of the books, the Edwards and the Cunningham-Prices, okay? If Edwards used any more of Cunningham-Price's books on which to base his own . . . then okay, I might admit you have something.'

'It's a deal.'

'But I'll bet you a pound that my man will be vindicated.'

Her eyes flashed. 'I don't gamble, Daniel. Remember?'

I nodded, chastised. Her ex-husband had been an inveterate gambler. 'Okay, sorry. But if Edwards used any more of Cunningham's ideas and characters, I'll buy you a Thai meal, okay?'

She nodded and shook my hand with pantomime seriousness. 'Deal,' she said.

. . .

My dear Vaughan, I exhort you, as a friend as well as your agent, to consider again your preoccupation with the occult. We're living in an increasingly rationalistic age. Readers don't go for this kind of thing any more. Charlesworth at Hutchinson is having second thoughts about commissioning the next book . . .

A letter from Desmond Maitland to Vaughan Edwards,
July 1980.

The following afternoon I dropped Mina at the hospital and took the road due north to Highdale.

It had rained continuously all day, a monsoon downpour that reduced visibility to less than twenty metres. In consequence I drove slowly, and the journey seemed to take an age. I usually listen to Radio 4 when driving, but that afternoon my thoughts were too full of Vaughan Edwards to concentrate on the play.

It was almost four o'clock when I pulled onto the cobbled square outside the White Lion. Evidently it had been market day; a few sodden traders were dismantling their stalls with a distinct lack of enthusiasm. I jumped from the car and ran across the cobbles to the public house, avoiding puddles but not the torrent that lashed down from a leaden sky.

A few more drinkers than last time were propped against the bar, and the publican greeted me with, 'Not fit for a dog out there. Orange juice?'

Surprised that he remembered me, I nodded. I pulled

the books from the inside pocket of my jacket. 'And I've returned these.'

He smiled as he fixed my drink. 'Hope you enjoyed them.'

I paid for the juice and carried it to the table beneath the bookshelf. Three volumes by E.V. Cunningham-Price, and nine by Edwards, still occupied the shelf. I pulled down the Cunningham-Prices and settled myself at the table. As with most Victorian novels, the date of publication was not given, though they had the look of books published in the last decade of the nineteenth century. I began speed-reading my way through, first, *Green Pastures*, and then *The Halfway House*.

Again and again I recognised turns of phrase, and sometimes entire descriptions, from those works of Edwards that I'd read. The plot of *Green Pastures* was pretty much recapitulated in Edwards' 1956 novel *Towards Sunset*. *The Halfway House* featured a character I recognised from one of his short stories.

And yet . . . I found it difficult to agree with Mina that Vaughan Edwards was a plagiarist. Certainly he had lifted from Cunningham-Price's work characters, descriptions, and certain lines – but from these he had fashioned his own unique novels, using, as it were, the original novels as a spring-board for his own im-agination. If anything, he could be said to have been collaborating with the earlier writer – even though it was a collaboration that had gone uncredited.

Then again, perhaps my love of his work would not allow me to accede to the charge that he was a plagiarist: in a court of law, the similarities between the two novelists' works would be sufficient evidence to have him declared guilty as charged.

I suppose the question now was, why had Vaughan Edwards used the works of E.V. Cunningham-Price as the starting point for so many of his own fictions? As a writer, and a voracious reader, I well understood that there were certain authors whose work was so over-whelmingly powerful, and which spoke to one's heart – irrespective of literary merit – that it was often difficult not to be influenced. But in my experience these influences were strongest when the writer was young and had yet to develop his or her own voice: with time one's vision matured, one's voice became wholly one's own . . . And yet Vaughan Edwards had clearly been influenced by Cunningham's work when working on his very last novel, *The Secret of Rising Dene*, published in 1996.

The affair had about it, in common with the man's life and disappearance, an air of insoluble mystery.

I turned my attention to the novels by Edwards, leafing through the volumes with that comfortable sense of anticipation that one inevitably acquires when handling unread books by favourite writers – and what if others might accuse him of plagiarism? I would argue with Mina that in Edwards' case the borrowings had been wholly justifiable, as they had helped to produce lasting works of literature.

The publican left the bar and made a tour of the snug, collecting empties. I took the opportunity to broach the subject of borrowing the books wholesale.

I held up a fifty-pound note. 'And I'll leave this until I return them,' I offered.

He frowned at the note, and laughed. 'You look like a gentleman and a scholar,' he said, not without humour. 'And you brought the others back. Take 'em. I'll trust you.'

He moved away, balancing half a dozen pint glasses along the length of his right arm.

I waited until the rain had let up slightly, then thanked the publican and hurried out to the car. I stowed the books on the passenger seat and started the engine, wondering what Mina might have to say when I arrived home with enough reading material for the next few weeks.

I drove from the square and up the hill, my progress impeded by a small truck which laboured up the incline. It was not until it approached the crest of the rise, and turned right through the ivied gateposts of Edgecoombe Hall, that I recognised the vehicle as the one parked by the Hall on my first visit.

On impulse I braked, then sat and watched as the truck disappeared into the gloom of the driveway.

It came to me that I could always pose as someone

interested in purchasing the tumbledown Hall, perhaps even ask the workman's permission to look around inside . . .

I turned down the drive and approached the Hall. The truck, parked around the corner as before, was emblazoned with the legend: Roy Giles, Builder. I saw a man, perhaps in his fifties, in baggy jeans and a red checked shirt, climb from the cab carrying a toolbox, and enter the building through a side door.

I braked and walked from the car, nervous now that the time had come to act the part of a prospective house buyer.

I rounded the corner and was approaching the side entrance when the man, presumably Giles, emerged.

'Can I help you?' Though his look was suspicious, his tone was friendly enough.

I gestured at the house. 'I was talking to the landlord of the White Lion,' I said. 'I hope to buy a place in the area. I don't suppose you know if it's for sale?'

'Matter of fact, I do.' He smiled. 'Chances are that it might be – but I won't know for sure for a year or so.'

He laughed at my puzzlement.

'Do you own the place?' I asked.

He scratched his head. 'Look, it's not as straightforward as all that.' He hesitated, considering. 'Why don't you come in and I'll explain.'

Bemused, I followed him through what I assumed

was the tradesman's entrance into an old scullery. It had been stripped bare and repainted; plumbing fixtures and fittings lay around the floor, evidence of recent work.

He gestured to the only seat in the room, a wooden sawing horse, and I sat down.

He brewed a pot of scalding black tea on a Calor gas stove and handed me a chipped mug. I sipped experimentally: it tasted far better than it appeared.

He leaned against the wall beside a window darkened by ivy, gripping his mug in both hands. 'It's a long story, but I'll make it short,' Giles said. 'I worked for the owner of the Hall for almost twelve years, you see. Odd job man, gardener, things like that. Then six years ago my employer vanished—' He clicked his thumb and forefinger. 'Snap. Just like that.' He shrugged. 'A few months later I was contacted by his solicitor. Imagine my surprise when I found out that the owner had made a will, leaving the Hall and all its contents to me. Thing was, no one was sure that Mr Edwards – the owner – was dead. Until his remains were discovered, or seven years had elapsed, then the Hall was technically still his property. Well, his remains have never been found, and he's been missing six years now. So . . . until next year, I don't rightly know if I'm the owner or not. I come in from time to time, do the odd bit of work here and there to keep the place from falling down.'

He looked at me. 'Not that I hope they find his

remains, understand? I'd be delighted if he walked back in here tomorrow.'

'Did you know him well?'

He frowned into his mug. 'Can't say that, but I respected him. He was a gentleman. He gave me work when I needed it and paid good money. He was a writer . . .' He shook his head and gave a wry smile. 'I tried one of his books once, but it wasn't my cup of tea.'

I nodded. 'It must have been quite a shock when he went missing?'

'To tell the truth, it wasn't. It wasn't so cut and dried. He'd been away from the Hall for a day or two when someone discovered his car in the woods, and footprints leading towards the river. The days passed, and I expected him to turn up at any time. I never really thought that he'd thrown himself over the scarp, and anyway no body was ever found, like I said. There was even a sighting of someone fitting Mr Edwards' description getting off a train at York.' He shrugged. 'It's a mystery what happened to him. I still sometimes think he'll walk in out of the blue.'

He laughed. 'So that's your answer. Come back in a year and I might be able to tell you one way or the other.'

I nodded, sipping my tea. 'It's not in the best of repair,' I began.

'I'll give you that,' he said. He hesitated, then went on: 'I'll show you around the place, if you like.'

He led the way from the scullery and down a long corridor, tripping light switches as he went. He flung open consecutive doors and stood aside to let me peer within, maintaining a running commentary as we went. 'Lumber room, still full of trunks and travelling cases.' And, 'Morning room, or that's what Mr Edwards called it, anyway.'

We came to a spacious hallway, illuminated by the light from a dusty chandelier, and crossed the chessboard tiles to a room he announced as, 'The study. This is where Mr Edwards wrote all his books.'

He flung open the door and switched on the light. I stepped inside, aware of my heartbeat. I was on the threshold of the room where Vaughan Edwards had created – with a little help from E.V. Cunningham-Price – his remarkable novels.

But for the film of dust that coated every horizontal surface, the room gave the appearance of still being in use. A typewriter sat on a desk by the ivy-choked window, and shelves of books lined the walls. A row of files – manuscripts, I guessed – occupied a bookshelf beside the desk. It was a pretty typical writer's study – the only thing missing being the writer himself.

My guide noticed me staring at the far wall, where a great crack in the brickwork, running from floor to ceiling, had been inexpertly plastered. I recalled the damage to the façade which I had noticed with Mina on our first visit, and the fissures in the grounds of the Hall.

'That's not the only one,' he said. 'I'll show you.'

He led me from the study and into the east wing of the house. There, in an empty room, he indicated yet another fissure that had been rendered over with discoloured plaster.

He opened a back door, which gave onto a spacious kitchen garden. He stepped out into the twilight and pointed to the rear wall of the building.

Along the length of the Hall, a series of great timber buttresses supported the bulging wall. The building seemed to bow outwards with the marked curvature of a galleon's hull; but for the sturdy props, the impression was that the Hall would have split open like an over-ripe fruit.

An ancient conservatory, with several panes of glass cracked or missing entirely, occupied the far end of the east wing.

'No doubt you'll have second thoughts about the place, now,' he said.

'Well, it does seem a bit tumbledown,' I ventured.

'Oh, it's surprisingly sturdy. These repairs were made a hundred years ago, and the place hasn't fallen down yet.'

The rain had abated, and in the light of the moon that appeared suddenly through the cloudrace I made out a series of crazed cracks in the garden – fissures that had been filled in over the years, but which still showed as slightly lower impressions radiating from the Hall itself.

'Mineshafts?' I asked at last. 'An underground stream?'

He looked at me and shook his head. 'An explosion.'

I stared at him. 'Explosion?'

'Well, that's what the locals said, those who were around at the time, and the story's passed into village folk lore.'

I turned and stared at the bulk of the house. Edgecoombe Hall was a dark shape against the moon-silvered clouds.

'What happened?' I asked.

'It's all a bit of a mystery. One night in December – this was in 1899 – a massive explosion was heard in the village. It came from up the hill – from Edgecoombe Hall. When a posse of locals arrived here, they saw a faint blue light hovering over the roof. The walls of the Hall were split open, and the ground all about was cracked.' He shrugged. 'The local bobby was called out and took a statement from the owner. That was the last of the affair, and there was no satisfactory explanation about what had happened.'

'Was the owner some kind of scientist? An experiment backfired?'

He laughed. 'He wasn't no scientist. He was a gentle-man landowner who wrote the odd novel.'

Quite involuntarily, the hair on the nape of my neck prickled, and a shiver ran down my spine. 'A writer?' I said.

'Gentleman by the name of Cunningham-Price,' my informant went on. 'Seems the Hall is popular with men of letters.'

'Cunningham-Price . . . ?'

I was not aware that I had uttered the name, and he stared at me. 'You've heard of him?'

'As a matter of fact I've read one of his books,' I managed. 'Quite a coincidence.'

My mind was racing. The coincidence that was uppermost in my thoughts, of course, was that Vaughan Edwards should have lived in the very same Hall, albeit many years later, as his literary hero. Then again, if he was so taken by Cunningham-Price's novels, what would be more natural than that he should seek out and purchase Edgecoombe Hall?

'Cunningham-Price was a bit of a recluse,' he was saying. 'Lived here alone, never married. Of course, after the explosion there was all manner of wild speculation and rumour. Locals swore he was deep into witchcraft, that the explosion was his attempt to summon the devil!'

'Has no one ever tried to work out scientifically what happened?' I asked.

'Not to my knowledge. That is, there's never been scientists in to investigate. Cunningham-Price hired some workmen to shore up the building – apparently he had them brick up the cellars.' He paused, looking at me. 'For what it's worth, I have a theory.'

I smiled. 'You do?'

'The area's riddled with underground streams and natural springs. It's a known fact that running water can accumulate static electricity. Perhaps a charge of electricity filled the cellar, reacted with something stored down there, and blew up.'

'And the blue glow that hung over the Hall?'

He shrugged. 'A result of the discharge – if a blue glow was present at all. We've only the word of the locals for that.'

He gestured inside, and we entered the Hall and made our way back to the scullery.

'What happened to Cunningham-Price?' I asked.

'He left the area around 1910. There was talk that he died in the First World War. The Hall was unoccupied for years, until Vaughan Edwards bought it in the mid-fifties. Two writers, one after the other' – he laughed – 'don't suppose you're another pen-pusher?'

'Computers,' I lied, my thoughts miles away.

He was writing his name and telephone number on a scrap of old wallpaper. He handed it to me. 'Like I said, I'll know how things stand in a year or so, if you'd like to get in touch.'

I hesitated before taking my leave. 'The landlord said the place is haunted,' I began.

He pulled his chin, nodding to himself. 'He's not wrong, either. Ghost of a young girl haunts the place – or should I say *haunted*?'

'But not any more?'

He shook his head. 'It left six years ago, around the time Mr Vaughan disappeared.'

I stared at Giles, wondering what Mina might have said to this. 'You believe in such things?'

He nodded, his expression stern, as if put out at my scepticism. 'You see, I saw the ghost – just the once. It was following Mr Vaughan up the main staircase, a blonde-haired girl as plain as daylight. And I'd often hear her laughter around the place. But, like I said, never since Mr Vaughan vanished . . .'

. . .

I know there is more to this reality than we perceive with our strictly limited senses; we are like new-born babies who have yet to acquire polychromatic vision, and see the world only in black and white. Beyond our conditioned purview of the world are wonders of which we cannot even dream . . .

From the novel *Seasons of Wonder* by Vaughan Edwards.

The return journey seemed to pass in no time at all, my thoughts full of the Hall's strange history, the two reclusive writers separated by years and yet so obviously connected by a similarity of the soul.

It was almost eight by the time I arrived home. Mina was not due back until ten, so I fixed myself a quick meal and settled beside the fire with the books I had brought from the White Lion.

I scanned the first of the Cunningham-Prices, *The White Lodge*, a story of a country house and its inhabitants over the course of thirty years. It had the unmistakable feel of something that Vaughan Edwards might have written, a haunting, elegiac quality, a sympathy for the characters, that was familiar from the modern writer's work . . . I had another seven of Edwards' books yet to read – it was quite possible that among the books I had taken from Highdale there would be one that borrowed, as I thought of it, from *The White Lodge*.

I was still reading when Mina arrived home. She made herself a cup of tea and collapsed with a sigh on the sofa next to me. She frowned at the pile of novels on the coffee table. 'So the day was a success?'

'And that's not all,' I said. I told her about my visit to the Hall and the conversation with Giles.

'Strange, or what?' I said.

She cupped her mug in both hands and sipped, eyeing me over the horizon of the rim. I could almost hear her mind working, practical as ever. 'What's so strange about it?' she asked.

I enumerated the strange points on my fingers. 'Cunningham-Price, a reclusive writer. The mysterious explosion. Cunningham-Price's unconfirmed death in the Great War. The ghost—'

Mina snorted at this. 'You've only the word of some cowboy builder about that!'

I shrugged. 'Nevertheless.' I held up my fingers. 'Vaughan Edwards, reclusive writer. He buys the place where his literary mentor lived and wrote. He uses the Victorian writer's novels as a starting point of his own—'

'So you admit he was a plagiarist?'

'Not in so many words.'

'But you're still going to buy me that Thai meal?'

'Very well. Will you stop interrupting?' I pulled back my thumb. 'Then Vaughan Edwards goes and disappears in mysterious circumstances.'

Mina sighed. 'Sometimes I wonder about you, Daniel. What's so strange? So Cunningham was a reclusive writer – so were you before you met me!'

'That's not fair.'

'The explosion – your builder chap explained that. And then Cunningham died in the war, along with millions of others. Vaughan Edwards comes along, buys the house of his hero, copies his novels, goes out for a walk one day and falls down the hillside, his body buried in undergrowth or snagged at the bottom of the river.' She smiled at me. 'And the ghost – show me an old English building that isn't rumoured to be haunted. Why look for bizarre explanations, Daniel, when the obvious answer is so straightforward?'

I shrugged. 'Sometimes the bizarre is more appealing than the everyday.'

'But wholly impossible,' she said. She ruffled my hair. 'Come on, let's go to bed.'

I followed her upstairs, trying to refute her cold water douche of rationalism – convinced, of course, that there was much more to the affair than met the eye.

. . .

It is all very well to drag the occult into his novels, but what this writer signally fails to realise is that the modern reader demands that the novelist provides also an interesting story . . .

> From Gerald Percival's review of *The White Lodge*
> by E.V. Cunningham-Price.

I read the Cunningham-Price books and the remaining Edwards novels over the course of the next fortnight. It came as no surprise to find that the Edwards borrowed heavily from the Cunningham-Prices. Minor characters in the Victorian novels cropped up in the modern novels as fully-fleshed protagonists. Themes hinted at in the early books were developed by Edwards and given full flight. Settings recurred, scenes, and even lines of dialogue.

I thought long and hard about what Edwards had done – a gifted novelist in his own right, he had no literary need to go about plundering someone else's work to use as the grist for his own books and stories. Except, of course, he obviously felt some kind of debt to the earlier writer – a duty to complete in his modern novels what the Victorian had left unsaid.

Weeks passed. I considered making my discovery

public in the form of an article, but if I approached a newspaper with my findings they would only request a sensationalist story of literary plagiarism spanning the years. I mulled over the idea of writing an essay for a small-press literary magazine, citing the examples of Edwards' borrowings and attempting to make a positive case for what he had done. At length I set the idea aside; it seemed to me that I had insufficient facts, that something was missing, information that might allow me to understand fully Edwards' objectives and motivations.

Life resumed its normal course, and I received the subtle impression that Mina was gratified that I had stepped down my search for the facts behind the story.

Not a day passed when I did not give thanks for having met her; I was beset less and less by the gnawing fear of her leaving me, a fear that in the early days of our relationship had often soured my peace of mind. We entered a period of mutual affection which I had never before known with anyone else, and I wanted to do nothing to undermine our happiness. I did not so much as mention Edwards, or Edgecoombe Hall. When I suggested that we dine at the Thai restaurant in Settle, I did so without reference to her having won our wager over Edwards' so-called plagiarism.

I received a commission to novelise a computer game, which I did over the next week or so and submitted under a pseudonym. Still I felt disinclined to embark upon an original novel, despite a phone call from my agent asking how it was coming along. I knew from experience that the creative drought would end in time, of its own mysterious accord, and in the meantime I would get by on hackwork. At the back of my mind, however, was the thought that apathy and laziness might win out, that I might never again want to write seriously enough to begin a project that meant something to me, a project I would have to invest with integrity and effort. The spectre of filling the years with hackwork in order to scrape a living hung over my waking days.

I forgot about Vaughan Edwards and the mystery of Edgecoombe Hall for long periods. On occasion, seeing the books that I would some day have to return to the White Lion, I did dwell on the events at Highdale and the strange case of his plagiarism – but I knew that the passage of years had all but quashed any chance of ever discovering the truth.

That might have been the case, but for the arrival through the post, a week later, of two novels which the editor of a small literary magazine wanted me to review.

• • •

I have never demanded from Mina the affection she obviously finds so hard to give to me. More than anything I want to ask her to show some sign that she . . . not that she loves me . . . but that she *cares*. But I'm terrified of asking that for fear of frightening her away.

From the personal journals of Daniel Ellis.

I was still in bed at nine-fifteen the following morning when Mina returned from taking the girls to school. She shouted up that she was preparing breakfast – and that the postman had just delivered a parcel of what looked suspiciously like books. The promise of breakfast might not have propelled me downstairs, but the arrival of post was assured to get me up.

Over fried eggs on Marmite toast, I opened the package and read the enclosed letter.

'Anything interesting?' Mina asked.

I indicated the two hardback books on the table, and lifted the note. 'The editor of *The Coastal Quarterly* wants me to review these. He read my piece on the last Boyd in the *Yorkshire Post*. Says he was impressed.'

'Great,' Mina said, 'but does he pay?'

'Trust your grubby little mind to think of nothing but filthy lucre. As a matter of fact,' I went on, 'he does.'

That stirred her interest. 'More Thai banquets?' she said.

'Hardly. He's offering me a fiver per book.'

'That's not much.'

'About what a small literary magazine can stretch to. I get thirty from the *Post*. The London periodicals usually pay fifty or so, but not some small-press imprint based in Whitby.'

I picked up the books. They were handsome first editions by a writer I'd never heard of, Ed Cunningham.

In retrospect, I was surprised the alarm bells didn't start ringing – but at the time I was oblivious to the tenuous connection.

Mina glanced across at me. 'You will review them, won't you?'

'Of course. I've got to keep you in Thai food, haven't I?'

Mina began work at ten, and after driving her to the hospital I brewed myself a coffee, lay on the sofa before the fire, and began reading *Sundered Worlds* by Ed Cunningham.

How to describe the shock of recognition, and the subsequent turmoil of emotions, that passed through my head as I read?

My pulse throbbed at my temple. My mouth ran suddenly dry and I felt light-headed.

Ed Cunningham . . .

I read on, my hands trembling.

Sundered Worlds was about a soldier invalided out of the army at the end of the First World War, and his fight to regain his physical and mental well-being at a sanatorium high in the Yorkshire Dales. There he met and fell in love with a young girl who, by the end of the novel, is revealed as the spirit of a girl murdered by Roundhead soldiers in the Civil War nearly three hundred years before . . .

Lines and turns of phrase echoed those in the works of E.V. Cunningham-Price and Vaughan Edwards.

A minor character in *Sundered Worlds* was none other than the central character in Cunningham-Price's *The White Lodge*.

Descriptions of the Yorkshire landscape eerily mirrored those of the earlier writers.

I finished the first book in three hours, and began the second, *Winter Harvest*.

Again and again: repeated lines, familiar characters, themes in common with the earlier books . . .

I read about the author on the back flap. There was no photograph, and the merest biographical information. Ed Cunningham was in his thirties and lived in the North Yorkshire town of Whitby. *Winter Harvest* was his second book. His first, *Sundered Worlds*, was now out in paperback.

I laid the books aside and stared into space, my mind dizzy with the impossible.

· · ·

God knows, there are times when my existence, what is happening to me, is more than I can humanly bear . . . and I desire nothing more than the balm of oblivion!

From the personal journals of E.V. Cunningham-Price.

'Daniel, are you okay?' She stood in the doorway of the front room, staring at me.

It was eight o'clock. The house was silent, and in

darkness. The girls were with Mina's ex-husband across town. I had no idea how long had passed since I had stopped reading.

She switched on the light and approached cautiously, as if at any second I might jump from the sofa and attack her.

'Daniel?'

I stared at her, shaking my head. I pointed to the books. 'They're the same,' I said. 'I should have known. Ed Cunningham.'

Mina sat beside me on the sofa and picked up the books.

'They contain lines and characters and descriptions from the other books,' I said.

She looked at me. I could see the practical cogs of her mind spinning a reply. 'So some hack discovered the plagiarism before you and he's doing his own take on it. It's all a big con.'

'How did they know?'

She sighed. 'How did *who* know?'

'Whoever sent the books. How did they know that I knew about Edwards and Cunningham?'

She reached out and ruffled my hair. 'Haven't you ever heard of coincidence, Daniel?'

'Massive bloody coincidence,' I said.

She pulled the editor's letter from one of the books, read it and then regarded me. 'Daniel, this was written two days ago.'

The course of her logic defeated me. I blinked. 'So?'

'So . . . two days ago was April fool's day.'

I shook my head, impressed, despite myself, by her dogged pragmatism. 'Fact remains, how the bloody hell did they know?' I paused. 'And it can't be a coincidence if it's an April fool's joke, can it?'

Touché. I saw her flinch.

A long silence came between us. Mina perched on the edge of the cushion, legs together, the letter open on her lap, her eyes downcast.

At last she said, 'I'm sure there's some perfectly logical explanation, Daniel.'

I wanted to hug her, to cherish her unfailing existential belief that was so much a part of her; at the same time I wanted to lash out at her in blind fury, angered by her inability to look beyond the mundane for fear of seeing something that might fill her with terror.

For a while, back in the darkness of the afternoon, my mind had glimpsed something that it had had no right to glimpse, and I was filled with a trembling fear of a myriad terrible possibilities.

'Daniel, I'm going to ring him.'

'Who?'

'Who do you think?' she said, lifting the letter. 'The editor of the magazine.'

'Is there a number?'

She scanned the letter-heading. 'Damn. No, but there's an address. I'll ring directory enquiries.'

She hurried into the hall. I heard the low, reassuring sound of her voice as she spoke into the receiver.

She returned a minute later. 'Strange. The magazine doesn't have a number.'

She sat down beside me. I took the letter, read the address. 'What's happening, Mina?'

She shook her head, brow drawn in furious thought. 'It's a practical joke, Daniel. Or it's a coincidence. It's one or the other. It can't be anything else.'

'Can't it?'

She snorted. 'What else can it be?'

I was silent for a long time. At last I said, 'Perhaps, just perhaps, E.V. Cunningham, Vaughan Edwards and Ed Cunningham are one and the same person.'

She *tsk'd* in scornful disbelief.

'Think about it! There's no record of Cunningham-Price's death, Vaughan Edwards vanished, and now these turn up – books that bear a remarkable resemblance to the earlier novels—'

'Daniel,' Mina pointed out with the sweet patience of a saint, 'if he were still alive he'd be . . . good God, I don't know . . . *ancient*.'

'At least a hundred and thirty, give or take,' I said.

'Somehow, I don't think so.'

I reread the address on the letter-heading.

'What?' Mina said, watching me.

'I'm going over there,' I said. 'I'll drop you off at the hospital tomorrow. Then I'll go over to Whitby, try to find out what's going on. According to the blurb, Ed Cunningham lives in Whitby—' I stopped.

'Daniel?'

'Perhaps this is his way of contacting me,' I said.

Mina stared at me for a long time, and I relented.

'Or then again,' I said, 'perhaps it is one big practical joke.'

I slept badly that night, and again and again reached out to touch Mina's reassuring warmth.

. . .

All we have, when all is said and done, for good or bad, is the constancy of our humanity.

From the novel *Summer in Ithaca* by Daniel Ellis.

The following day at ten I dropped Mina off at the hospital.

She had been quiet for the duration of the drive, but before she climbed from the car she gave me an unaccustomed peck on the cheek and said, 'I hope you find the joker, Daniel. Take care, okay?'

I nodded and drove away.

Bright sunlight alternated with silvery showers as I took the long, high road over the North Yorkshire moors towards Whitby. I considered the events of the past few months, the strange occurrences at the Hall, the odd plagiarism that now connected three writers spanning as many centuries. I told myself that I had always kept an open mind as regards phenomena considered . . . let's say . . . *bizarre,* but now I felt that I was fast approaching someone who might be able to answer some of my many questions, and quite frankly I was more than a little apprehensive.

The sky over the North Sea was as leaden as the ocean itself as I came to the crest of the road and looked down on the bay and the tumbling town of Whitby. The sun was concealed behind a bank of cloud the colour of old bruises; the scene was drear and inhospitable, and I could well imagine why Bram Stoker had chosen as Dracula's point of arrival in England this grey and unprepossessing fishing port.

The address given on the note-paper was in the village of Throxton, a few miles north of Whitby on the coast road. I drove slowly, anxious now that the time had come to approach the man who had sent me the Cunningham books for review. He had signed himself as Gerald Melthem, the literary editor of *The Coastal Quarterly*.

What if Mina was right, and the whole affair was no more than a massive and unlikely coincidence? How might I explain myself to the editor then?

I decided to broach that eventuality if and when it occurred.

But if it were not a coincidence, then what might it be?

Throxton was a hamlet consisting of a dozen large houses strung out along the clifftop beside the coast road. I came upon Hapsley House quite by accident. I slowed and braked before the first big house in the village, intending to ask directions, and was surprised to read on a cross-section of tree-trunk, affixed to the gate, the title: Hapsley House.

The rain had abated, and the sun was out again. A mist hung over the road, and when I stepped from the car, my heart beating like a trip-hammer, I found that the afternoon was unseasonably mild.

I opened the gate and approached the front porch, only to be informed by a hand-written sign that visitors should ring at the side entrance.

I walked around the tall, grey-stone building, past rhododendron bushes spangled with rain, and found the side door.

Before I knocked, I heard the sound of a child's laughter emanating from the rear garden, and when I looked I saw, obscured by a stand of apple trees, the distant sight of a tall man in a white shirt, pushing a radiantly blonde girl in a swing. She was perhaps fifteen or sixteen, and her uninhibited laughter, as it carried over the garden on the sea wind, brought suddenly to mind the long gone summers of my youth.

I remembered myself, and rang the bell.

Almost immediately the door was opened by a grey-haired woman dressed in the old-fashioned garb of a housekeeper or maid. She looked at me severely, as if unaccustomed to receiving callers.

'Can I help you?'

'I've come to see Mr Melthem.'

She appeared unmoved, so I continued, 'If you could tell him that Daniel Ellis wishes to see him.'

She said, 'Are you a writer?' as if admission to this might prove the open sesame.

I nodded. 'Mr Melthem sent me some books to review.'

'In that case do come in, Mr Ellis. Please, follow me.'

She closed the door behind me and led the way up a narrow flight of stairs to a long room overlooking the sea. The lounge was stuffed with too much old-fashioned furniture, cabinets full of china, and an abundance of chintz.

'One moment while I inform Mr Melthem . . .' She left the room, and I moved to the window and stared out.

The tall man – I would guess that he was in his sixties – was leaning against the iron frame of the swing and talking to the girl. Even at this distance I was overcome with her Alice-like beauty; something in her laughing manner filled me with delight.

The housekeeper came into view in the garden beneath me and called to the man. He turned and looked up at the window where I stood, and involuntarily I took a backwards step so as to be out of sight.

When next I looked, the man was striding up the

garden path towards the house, but of the young girl there was no sign.

A minute later I heard footsteps on the stairs, and the door opened suddenly.

He stood at the far end of the room for a second, lost in the shadows, as if assessing me. Then he strode forwards, his hand outstretched.

Closer to, I could see that he was much older than I had first assumed. Though he held himself stiffly upright with an almost military correctitude, the skin of his face and hands had the tissue-thin, translucent quality of great age.

I reached out to take his hand, my own trembling. I recalled the dream I had had, several months ago, of meeting a writer in an ancient library – and how I had been convinced, upon awakening, that the writer had been Vaughan Edwards.

The man before me bore an uncanny resemblance to the hazy figure in my dream . . .

'Mr Ellis,' he said warmly. 'Please, take a seat.' He indicated a wicker chair beside the window and took one positioned opposite, a wicker table between us.

The housekeeper appeared at the door, and Melthem asked me, 'A drink? Tea, coffee?'

'Tea, black,' I said.

The old man said, 'I have enjoyed your novels, Mr Ellis. They embody a spirit, let's say an attitude of mind, not often found in these modern times.'

I shrugged, at a loss. I always find flattery, on the infrequent occasions it is directed my way, more difficult to handle than criticism.

'That's kind of you. I try to write what I find most important to me.'

He sighed. 'Don't we all, Mr Ellis?' he said.

'You write yourself?' I asked, idiotically.

His reply was interrupted by the arrival of the housekeeper with our tea. Meltham poured the Earl Grey into two improbably delicate china cups.

I took mine on a saucer, the china chattering a quick signal of my nervousness.

Only then did I notice, on the table between us, a slim book. It was the collection of Vaughan Edwards' short stories – *Improbable Visions* – that I had yet to read.

I wondered if Mina would call this a coincidence, too?

My vision misted and my head reeled. I thought, for a second, that I was about to collapse. The feeling passed. I sipped my tea.

'I take it you received the Cunninghams?' he enquired.

I nodded. 'Yesterday. I've read them already. I was . . . impressed. They show a mature handling of character and situation—' I was aware that I was gabbling, running off at the mouth. 'A maturity surprising for a novelist's first books . . .'

'Quite. Exactly my feelings, too. I thought you might

appreciate them. Isn't it wonderful to happen upon like souls in the appreciation of the noble art?'

I smiled and gulped my tea.

He noticed my glance towards the Vaughan Edwards collection. 'A gift,' he said, and an icy hand played a rapid arpeggio down my spine. 'I thought you might appreciate the volume.'

I thanked him with a whispered, '. . . most kind.' And took refuge behind my cup.

How had he known I would come here, I wanted to shout: for that matter, how did he know that this of all Vaughan Edwards' books was the one I had yet to read?

I felt as though I were participating in a dream over which I had no control, and from which I might at any second awake in fright.

'I was at Edgecoombe Hall just the other day,' Melthem was saying.

I nodded, at a loss quite how to respond. I sat rooted to my seat, my posture rigid, staring at him as he said, 'Would you care to meet me tomorrow at the Hall, between eleven and noon?'

I found myself assenting with a gesture.

'Splendid. There is so much to explain, and it would help if we were in the Hall where it all originally happened, don't you think?'

'Cunningham-Price, Edwards . . . ?' It was barely a whisper, a feeble attempt to articulate the many questions crowding my mind.

'Tomorrow, Mr Ellis.'

He reached out a papery hand, and when I looked into his sapphire-blue eyes it came to me that I was in the presence of someone who had experienced more than it was humanly possible to experience, and still survive.

The feeling was gone almost as soon as it arrived. I found myself shaking his hand. I rose from the chair and gestured farewell.

'Oh, Mr Ellis . . .' He called out as I made for the door. He held the volume of short stories towards me. I murmured an apology and took the book.

As I reached the door, he said, 'Tomorrow, between eleven and noon, Mr Ellis. I'll see you at Edgecoombe Hall.'

In a daze I hurried down the stairs and let myself out through the side door. The fresh air seemed to waken me, as if from the dream I had been so convinced I had fallen into. I made my way to the car, regretting now that I had not remained to question him – but at the same time not wishing in the slightest to return.

I made a three-point turn and accelerated up the road towards Whitby. As I came to the rise above the hamlet, I glanced back at the imposing grey pile of Hapsley House. I slowed the car and stopped, turning in my seat and staring.

Melthem had returned to the garden overlooking the

sea, and once again he was pushing the laughing, golden-haired girl on the swing.

Sweating, I turned my back on Hapsley house and drove away.

· · ·

> Do I love him? What is love? Do I trust him? If trust is giving your fate to another, and knowing that you will not be harmed, then I trust him. But do I love him? After The Bastard, how can I bring myself to love anyone? So why, then, do I trust him?
>
> From the diary of Mina Pratt.

I arrived home at six. Mina was still at work. I was relieved to have the house to myself. I would have found it hard to find rational answers to her questions; indeed, I found it hard myself to answer the many questions posed by the events of that afternoon.

I built the fire, taking my time with wadded newspapers, sticks of wood, coal and fire-lighters. I have always found the act of making a fire comforting, therapeutic. With the fire blazing, I sat on the sofa and considered eating – but I had no appetite.

I fetched *Improbable Visions* from my jacket where it hung in the hall, and returned to the front room. I resumed the sofa and began reading: the act seemed appropriate.

Mina returned at eight. The sound of the front door opening brought me back to reality. I was aware of my heartbeat, and the fact that I was not looking forward to facing her.

She appeared in the doorway and paused, gripping a bulky carrier bag of groceries. She stared at me. 'What happened, Daniel?'

I could not bring myself to reply. She disappeared into the kitchen, and I heard the sound of her unpacking the shopping and storing it away in cupboards. It struck me as the typical, practical thing that Mina would do at a time like this.

She emerged five minutes later, again halting in the doorway as if wary of approaching me. 'Are you going to tell me what happened?'

I found my voice at last. 'I met him,' I said.

She nodded. 'The editor?'

I could not bring myself to look at her. Instead I regarded the leaping flames. I licked my lips.

'Edwards,' I said. 'Or Cunningham-Price, or whatever he calls himself.'

The flames danced. Mina said nothing. The silence stretched painfully. I tore my eyes away from the fire and looked at her.

She was staring at me, and slowly shaking her head. She said, 'He told you he was Edwards?'

'No, not in so many words—'

'Then just what did he say?' I could hear the exasperation in her tone.

'It was strange, Mina. The meeting seemed unreal,

like a dream. I wanted to ask so much, but I found myself unable to form the questions. He told me very little.'

'Then how on earth did you know he was Edwards?' she almost cried.

I shook my head. 'A feeling, an intuition. He was so old. At first I thought he was about sixty, seventy. Then . . . I don't know. When he spoke, when I looked into his eyes, I realised he was ancient.'

Mina moved to the armchair before the fire. She pulled her feet onto the cushion and hugged her shins, staring at the flames.

She glanced at me. 'Did you ask him why he sent the books?'

I shook my head. 'I think he wanted to communicate with me . . . tell someone about himself, after all those years.'

'But you said he told you next to nothing!'

My mouth ran dry. I considered my words. 'I think he wants to explain, tell someone who might be sympathetic. He said he liked my books, sympathised with their sentiments—'

'Wants to explain?' she asked, a note of what might have been apprehension in her voice. 'You're meeting him again?'

I nodded. 'He wants to meet me at Edgecoombe Hall tomorrow. He said that there's much to explain.'

'And you're going?'

I let the silence stretch, become almost unbearably tense, before it snapped and she asked, 'Well?'

I looked up at her, held her gaze. 'I've got to go, Mina. I want to find out.'

She gave a quick, bitter shake of her head and stared at the flames.

'Mina, something strange and wonderful happened at the Hall all those years ago . . . All my life I've been hoping that there was more to . . . to *this* . . . than what is apparent. We're so programmed by our limited perceptions and this reality's conditioning. There's more to existence than what is apparent to the senses. There has to be. If this is all there is, then I'd despair . . .'

She turned her head and stared at me, and I was shocked to see something almost like hatred in her eyes. 'You're a fool, Daniel. You're a bloody fool! Can't you be satisfied with what there is? Why all this searching?'

'I don't know.'

'Isn't what you've got enough?' She said this with her eyes downcast, unable to look at me.

I almost replied, then, cheaply, that if she would give me all her love, then that might be enough – but I held my tongue. 'It isn't about what I've got,' I said. 'It's about what's possible.'

'Listen to me, the editor is a con man – he's planning something.'

'He knew I was coming,' I interrupted, indicating the collection. 'He had this for me, the only Vaughan Edwards I haven't read. He knew that.'

'Impossible!'

'Another coincidence?' I sneered.

A silence developed, and the fire hissed and cracked. At last Mina said, 'Are you going?' in a small voice.

'What do you think? I've got to go. I must find out what's happening.'

Suddenly, surprising me, Mina stood and moved to the door. 'I'm meeting Liz at nine,' she said. 'We're going for a drink. You can fix your own dinner, can't you?'

The mention of such banalities angered me, but she hurried from the doorway and was climbing the stairs before I could reply.

I sat in silence, staring at the glowing coals.

She came down thirty minutes later, dressed in her short black coat, the collar turned up around her wind-swept-effect hair. She looked wonderful, and a part of me wanted to take her in my arms and apologise and tell her that I would not be going to Highdale in the morning.

I remained seated.

'Daniel,' she said, and I could tell that she had been giving the words great thought, 'I won't be back to-night. I'm staying over at Liz's.'

I nodded. 'Have a good time.'

She did not move from the door. 'So you're going up there, then?'

'That's what I said, isn't it?'

'I wish you wouldn't, Daniel,' she said, and made to leave.

I stopped her with, 'What do you fear, Mina?'

'What's that supposed to mean?'

'Do you care about what might happen to me, or fear I might discover something that might shatter your safe, limited little world view?'

She stared at me, slowly shaking her head. 'I don't have the slightest idea what you're talking about—'

'It's the latter, isn't it? You don't want your safe, cosy existence shattered by the knowledge that there's more to life than merely this . . .' I gestured about me . . . 'this physical existence. I've never met anyone as closed-minded as you.'

She could only stare at me, tears filming her eyes. 'That's not fair. I do care . . .'

I could not help myself. 'You've got a damned strange way of showing it, then. I know you've told me, again and again, that you don't love me . . . but what about affection?'

'Daniel . . .'

'Is it simply that you don't trust me, after all the love and affection I've shown you? Is that it? You know, never once in the year we've been together have you shown any spontaneous sign of intimacy. It's always me who has to make the first move. Do you know how galling that is? Do you ever stop to wonder what it's like to love someone, and not to have the slightest clue as to what the hell they feel about you in return?'

She was crying now, leaning against the door-frame and sobbing.

I twisted the knife. 'I sometimes wonder why the hell you bother staying with me!'

Shocked and angered, she looked up and stared at me, and I knew I had gone too far then, and would regret it. 'If that's how you feel . . .' she wept.

She hurried into the hall.

'What?' I called after her.

I heard the front door open. Then, suddenly, she was back, framed in the doorway, staring at me. 'You bastard,' she said. 'Don't expect me to be here when you get back.'

And, before I could reply, she was gone.

Three

As a child I read a lot, lost myself in adventures and quests along with characters more real than anyone I had ever met in real life. Books were my refuge, a bolt-hole to other, better worlds than this one, an escape.

Perhaps they served much the same function now, though on a more sophisticated level: now I might lose myself in a book to escape the exigencies of this life, but at the same time fiction was a way of understanding others, of realising that one's own psychological view-point was not the only one. By engaging with the diversity and variation of thought and character to be found in literature, I was making my own life richer and more rewarding.

Vaughan Edwards' books had fulfilled both the above criteria; they had offered me a brief escape from this reality, and a means of understanding another person's unique world view. For me, the bizarre, other-worldly tales they told functioned as a grand metaphor for something very strange.

And I wanted to experience that strange reality for myself.

I awoke late the following morning in a bed cold without Mina. I forced myself to drink a cup of coffee, and at ten set off for Highdale.

As I drove, I considered Mina's declaration that she would not be at home when I returned. I decided that later, when I had met Vaughan Edwards – or whoever he might be – I would seek out Mina, and apologise. I could always tell her that I had acceded to her wishes, and not gone to the Hall.

But lies breed a subsequent duplicity, the need to follow up the original untruth with a series of others. I had never lied to Mina, and I did not want to begin now: what I was doing meant something to me – even though I was filled with apprehension at the same time – and I knew that it would devolve to me, upon my return, to attempt to explain this to Mina, somehow make her understand. If she were to share my life, then she must also share my mind. Relationships are founded on mutual understanding, and how could our partnership work if she failed to comprehend what the mystery of Vaughan Edwards and Edgecoombe Hall meant to me?

I arrived at Highdale just as cloud cover occluded the sun and a squall of heavy rain began. I drove past the Hall and into the village, glad of the excuse to delay the inevitable encounter: I had brought back the books I had borrowed from the White Lion on my last visit.

It was just after eleven when I pushed into the snug and returned the novels to their shelf. I was tempted to delay the rendezvous still further by ordering a drink, but resisted the urge. The sooner I learned the truth of Edgecoombe Hall, I reasoned, the sooner I could return to Mina.

I left the pub and drove slowly up the hill. The rain was torrential now, making ineffectual the laboured swipes of the windscreen-wipers. I slowed to a walking pace, hunching over the wheel so as to make out the road ahead.

I came to the ivied gateposts and turned, feeling as I did so the oppressive weight of something very much like fear settle over me. It was not, I told myself, too late to turn back. I could retreat now and be back home inside the hour, and I would be able to tell Mina that I had not set eyes on Edgecoombe Hall that day.

Even as I considered this option, I knew that I would not take it. I had set out with the express intention of meeting with Vaughan Edwards, if such was who he was, and I could not at this late stage deny myself the opportunity of discovering the truth.

By the time I emerged from the tunnel of shrubbery, the rain had abated, and the sun appeared from behind the clouds. Edgecoombe Hall stood before me, presenting an even more inimical façade for being so theatrically bathed in sudden sunlight.

I braked the car and remained inside for long minutes, aware that I was gripping the steering wheel as the survivor of a shipwreck might cling to flotsam. My pulse hammered at my temple, and sweat soaked my shirt.

I climbed from the car and approached the Hall, unsure now the time had come whether to knock on the main door or try the side entrance.

There was no sign of another vehicle: perhaps, I told myself, he had not yet arrived.

As I stood, momentarily paralysed by indecision, I heard a familiar sound from within the building.

The high joyous trill of a young girl's uninhibited laughter issued from the dour precincts of the Hall, a sound as golden as the sunlight without.

I attempted to peer through those windows not obscured by ivy, but what little I could make out of the interior was lost in shadow.

Then the great timber front door opened, and instantly the girl's laughter ceased.

He stood upon the top step, smiling down at me – and again I received the impression of great age and amiability.

'Mr Ellis, Daniel – splendid that you could make it.'

His face was thin, his hair gun-metal grey, and though there was about him a suggestion of infirmity –

in the slight stoop of his frame, as opposed to his ramrod posture of yesterday – yet he seemed to glow with a lustrous vitality.

I found myself saying, quite unrehearsed, 'Who are you?'

He smiled, not at all put out by the question. 'Daniel, I think you know that by now, don't you?' It was almost a laugh.

I cleared my throat, began, 'You . . . are you—?' I halted, unable, for some reason, to bring myself to say the name.

He came to my assistance. 'I am Edward Vaughan Cunningham-Price, to give me my somewhat long-winded title.'

I opened my mouth to speak, but remained inarticu-late.

He smiled. 'Would you care to come inside?'

I stood rooted to the spot, quite unable to move.

At last I said, 'What happened in '96, and before that, in the Great War?'

He considered my question. 'In '96 it was necessary for me to move on, and likewise before that in 1916—'

'How,' I said, hearing my words as if from a great distance, '. . . how old are you?'

He nodded, as if this were a perfectly reasonable question. 'I am one hundred and seventy-eight, Daniel.'

He peered into the sky; a cloud scudded across the

sun, suddenly darkening the Hall. 'I think rain is on the way. You'll catch your death if you remain out there. Do come in.'

He stood back and gestured with an outstretched hand for me to enter. He was the epitome of genial hospitality, and for some reason it came to me that, despite everything, I could trust him.

I mounted the steps one by one. At the top I paused, facing him. 'How is that possible?' I murmured.

He laid a hand on my arm. 'Daniel, that is what I came here to explain. Please, this way . . .'

He turned and walked into the Hall. I followed him across the chessboard tiles, down a long corridor towards the back of the house. From time to time he made comments over his shoulder about the weather, and asked me if the drive up had been pleasant, as if such mundane smalltalk might put me at ease.

A part of me expected to see the laughing girl dancing in delight somewhere in the Hall. And yet, at the very same time, some intuitive part of my consciousness knew that she would not appear.

We passed though a double glass door, and for a second I thought that we were stepping outside: then I found myself in a vast conservatory, quite denuded of vegetation.

I looked around, bemused. I had expected to be shown something – I have no idea what – but the great glassed-in area was empty.

Cunningham-Price moved to the centre of the floor and stooped, lifting the ring of a trap-door to reveal a flight of steps descending into darkness. He took three steps down, then turned and smiled at me to follow.

'Where . . . where are we going?'

'The cellar, Daniel.'

I recalled what the builder, Giles, had told me weeks ago. 'The cellar? He – you . . . you had the cellar bricked up after the explosion.'

'All but this entrance,' he explained.

'What happened?' I asked. 'The explosion – what was it?'

He paused, regarding me. 'I was writing in my study at the time. It was late, midnight if I recall. The explosion shook the very foundations of the Hall. I made my way into the cellar, through the entrance in the scullery. I . . .' He paused, his vision misting over as he recalled the events of over one century ago. 'I beheld a remarkable sight, Daniel.'

I heard myself whisper, 'What?'

'It was the arrival here of something unique in the history of humankind,' he said, and continued down the steps.

My heart hammering, God help me, I followed.

We came to the foot of the steps. A naked bulb gave a feeble light, illuminating a short corridor, at the end of which was a door. Cunningham-Price paused before it, took a key from his pocket and turned it in the lock.

He looked at me over his shoulder. 'I would advise you to shield your eyes,' he counselled.

Puzzled, and not a little apprehensive, I did so, peering out beneath my hand as he turned the handle and eased open the door.

An effulgent glow, like the most concentrated lapis lazuli, sprang through the widening gap and dazzled me. I think I cried out in sudden shock and made to cover my eyes more securely. When I peered again, Cunningham-Price was a pitch black silhouette against the pulsing illumination as he stepped into the chamber.

Trembling with fright, I followed. As I crossed the threshold I heard, for the first time, a constant dull hum, as of some kind of dynamo, so low as to be almost subliminal.

I stepped inside and, as my vision grew accustomed to the glare, removed my hand from my eyes and peered across the chamber.

How to describe what I saw, then?

It seemed to me that, embedded in the far wall, was a great orb of dazzling blue-white light – like a swollen will-o'-the-wisp. It was as bright as the sun seen with the naked eye, and seemed to be spinning, constantly throwing off crazed filaments of crackling electricity; these filaments enwebbed the chamber, flowing around the walls and totally encapsulating us as we stood there in mute awe. Only then, belatedly, did I realise that the chamber was not a cellar room as such, but more like a cave, a great cavern excavated perhaps by the force of the explosion all those years ago.

'What . . .' I managed at last, 'what is it?'

In lieu of a reply, he said, 'When I heard the explosion I came down here forthwith – don't ask me how I knew its location. It was as if I were drawn here. I made my way cautiously down the stairs, afraid but at the same time unable to resist the impulse to investigate. Then suddenly I came upon this light occupying the space where my wine cellar had once been . . .'

He stopped there, a sad light in his eyes, as if the thought of what had happened then was too much. 'I . . . I have no idea how long I was down here. It seemed like hours, but later it came to me that only a matter of minutes had elapsed.'

He paused again, and I waited. I stared into the pulsating will-'o-the-wisp like someone hypnotised, then tore my gaze away and looked at him.

'And then?' I prompted.

'And then,' he went on, 'they communicated with me.'

I stared at him, at once wanting to disbelieve his bizarre story and yet, because of the very evidence of my eyes, unable to do so.

'They?' I echoed.

'Or perhaps I should say "she",' he said. 'At least, that was the form they took to approach me. You see,' he went on, 'I was writing a novel at the time, about a soldier's love for a young girl . . . And they reached into my mind, and took this image of the child, and used it.' He paused there, on the verge of tears, his face drawn as he recalled the events of more than a century ago.

Seconds elapsed. A dizzy nausea gripped me. My conscious mind was exhorting me to run, to get out and never return, and yet at the same time another part of me, that part forever fascinated with the lure of the arcane, wanted nothing more than to hear the conclusion to his story.

He faced the light, tears now streaming down his cheeks. 'She came to me from the light, a fair innocent child emanating such an aura of purity that I was overcome. She explained that she was from elsewhere, that her kind had opened a channel from her realm to this world, and that they wished to study us . . .'

I said, 'Aliens? Beings from another dimension?'

He shook his head. 'Neither description quite fits the reality,' he said. 'She tried to make clear to me the nature of their realm, but my human mind, conditioned only to accept this world, could not begin to comprehend the place from whence she came. It was not from outer space, or from another dimension, or an alternate world – it was from a place that existed beyond matter as we understand it. Her universe was one of energy without physical form, and she herself consisted of pure energy. She, or it, or whatever, was bemused by the discovery of this world, and wanted to understand.'

He wept. 'The girl . . . It was as if she had the power to demand from me all the love, all the compassionate desire, I had ever felt for anyone. I stood before this ethereal creature and I was besotted. I could but accede to her desire . . .'

Something surged within me, a sudden, terrifying panic.

'What?' I began. 'What did she want?'

He forced his gaze away from the effulgence as if with great effort, and faced me, sobbing uncontrollably now and shaking his head.

As I stared at him, something in his lean, aquiline face altered. The lineaments of age seemed to dissolve, become suffused with a golden glow. I stepped backwards in alarm as the form of a young girl – the very girl I had beheld in the garden at Throxton – took shape within the old man and then stepped out, smiling at me.

Something hit me then, the full force of this creature's irresistible allure, and I cried out in rapture.

Behind her, Cunningham-Price, divested of energy, slumped suddenly, and in that second he seemed to age a hundred years.

I backed away, came up against the cavern wall.

The girl regarded me, smiling with angelic sweetness. It was hard to believe that she was a mere manifestation of pure energy, a being from another dimension; she seemed to possess, in her radiant form, the essence of all womanly pulchritude and sensuality.

'I wanted to dwell within the being of Cunningham-Price,' she said. 'He was a writer, and I was intrigued by his visions; more, by his heightened emotions. I had never before experienced such feelings, such emotion. I wanted to inhabit him.'

'You wanted to take him over!' the rational side of my mind protested.

'I would grant him powers of which he had never dreamed,' the girl continued. 'I would bestow upon him increased longevity, allow him to live beyond the paltry duration you poor beings are allotted. I would give him perfect health, and new abilities. He would have intuition as none of you might know, and foresight, and the ability to shape circumstances to his will . . .'

A sudden, dreadful realisation came to me. 'The books,' I began. 'He knew I was coming!'

She smiled, and the quick knowing look that crossed her face filled me with sudden panic. 'All along . . .' I cried. 'If he could shape circumstances . . .' My mind reeled, and I felt utterly powerless before this lambent being.

'Why?' I managed. 'What do you want?'

'Cunningham-Price is old,' she said. 'There is only so much that even I might do to sustain and prolong the life of the flesh. He is unable to host me any longer. I require someone with his sensibilities, with his innate understanding of what it is to be human, someone in contact with their emotions. We read your books, Daniel. We knew you were the one.'

She stepped forward. Behind her, Cunningham-Price fell to the floor like a dead weight.

I cried out in an anguish of dilemma. I was overcome with a tidal wave of desire, the need to lavish upon this creature all the love I had within me, even though I knew that she was manipulating this desire. I wanted to love the girl as I loved Mina – but, even as I realised this, I knew too that the girl would be unable to reciprocate: what did this creature of energy know of the very attribute unique to the human race? She would inhabit me and use me, and I would live an extended life in thrall to this supernal creature, forever in love, while she would study me like some laboratory specimen, without the need or desire to love me in return.

I cried out. I wanted to take the easy option and step towards her, allow her to inhabit my being. I would be free then of the tangled web of emotions that make human relationships so terribly difficult. I would be her slave, and a part of me desired the ease of worshipping at the altar of her beauty.

And yet . . . and yet, what made human relations so joyous, so fulfilling, was that the effort of loving was often rewarded, that effort expended was sometimes repaid, or at least we live in hope that our need to be needed might find in someone, somewhere, a like need . . .

I dived away from her outstretched hands. I fell to the floor and scrambled in the direction of the door. I heard her coaxing, mocking laughter trilling behind me, but I dared not bring myself to look back in case I weakened and allowed her entry.

On all fours I lunged at the door, hauling myself upright, flinging it open and running. I stumbled again and again, crying out as I imagined, at any second, to feel the warmth of her energy flow into me. Again and again I picked myself up, flung myself up the flight of stairs, my arms and legs bruised and painful, my heart labouring fit to burst. I came to the conservatory, the full moon silvering the panes of glass all around me, and without a backward glance ran through the darkened Hall in the direction of the entrance.

I hauled open the front door and bolted into the night. My car, a welcome symbol of banal modernity, stood where I had left it before the house. I dived into the driver's seat and started the engine – miraculously it fired first time – then steered in a crazy, careering u-turn and accelerated away from the Hall.

I did not look back – a fear like I had never known before would not allow me to turn my head to check if I was being pursued, even though every fibre of my being wanted to do so.

I sped from the Hall, down the hill away from the

woodland. I wondered at the creature's range, its ability to chase me until I was caught. I told myself that, the greater distance I was able to put between myself and Edgecoombe Hall, the safer I would be. It had not, after all, possessed me when it had had the chance back in the cavern. Perhaps my headlong flight had saved my soul . . .

Still I accelerated, taking corners at breakneck sped, with no care at all for my safety, pursued as I imagined myself to be by a far, far greater danger.

I failed to see the oncoming vehicle until it was too late. Its glaring headlights appeared around the corner as if from nowhere, and instinctively I hauled on the wheel. My car careered from the road, bucked over a banking and rolled down what seemed like a never-ending incline. By the time it reached the bottom and halted, on its side, broken glass tinkling around me in a strangely beautiful glissando, my consciousness was rapidly ebbing away.

Seconds later I passed into oblivion.

. . .

There are times when I give thanks for what has happened to me, knowing that I am unique among all men; there are other times, however, when I feel the curse of this possession. To give love that cannot be returned, and to be denied the opportunity to exhibit love for any other . . .

From the personal journals of Vaughan Edwards.

I came awake to find myself slung on my side, cradled by the seat-belt. My body was frozen, and an intense pain gripped my head and legs. I waited, trapped, for the girl to find me, to take me over. I cried aloud in anguish at my inability to flee. I thought of Mina, and wanted nothing more than to apologise.

I passed out.

And awoke . . . to find myself in bed, and warm, the pain no more than a distant memory. I recall crying out in fear, and a soothing hand upon my forehead, before falling unconscious yet again.

The next time I came awake, I had a raging thirst. I tried to find the words to communicate my desire for water, but the effort was beyond me. I tried again, what seemed like hours later, and was rewarded. A disembodied hand – I could not move my head to see who it belonged to – lifted a beaker of water to my lips, and I drank.

Between moments of fleeting consciousness, I dreamed. I was in the cellar, and the girl-creature was reaching out, and I felt again the desire to give this being all the love that I possessed, and then it came to me with even more intense terror that that love could never be returned.

I awoke once in darkness, the hospital quiet around me, and the more I thought about the events at the Hall, the more I came to doubt the truth of what had happened . . .

Then I recalled, crying quietly to myself, what Mina had told me the last time I had seen her: that she would not be there for me when I returned from Edgecoombe Hall.

When I awoke again, it was morning. Intense sunlight cascaded through a window. A vase of brilliant daffodils seemed the most miraculous sight I had ever witnessed.

I felt a hand take mine, and squeeze.

With incredible effort, I moved my head, and the reward was worth the pain.

Mina sat beside the bed, smiling at me through her tears.

'You fractured your skull,' she reported in a small voice, 'broke both your legs. You were in a coma for a week. They thought—' She stopped herself, dried her eyes with a Kleenex. 'They thought you might not survive.'

I gripped her fingers. 'I'm sorry,' I said.

'Daniel,' she whispered, after a long silence, 'what happened?'

I shook my head. 'I don't know,' I said. 'I really don't know . . .'

A nightmare, I thought . . .

She smiled at me, and I slipped into unconsciousness.

She was by my side when I awoke again, maybe hours later. She was staring at a newspaper, her expression shocked.

'What is it?' I asked.

'Daniel, look . . .'

She held up the *Yorkshire Post*. The front-page head-line declared: MISSING NOVELIST DISCOVERED DEAD.

'Vaughan Edwards,' she reported. 'He was found yesterday in the cellar of the Hall. He'd died of a heart attack. They give his age here as seventy-two.' She lowered the paper and smiled at me, shaking her head. 'All those crazy ideas of yours . . .'

I smiled at her. 'I was a fool,' I said.

I watched her, and wondered what had really happened at the Hall; had it all, actually, been nothing more than a figment of my overwrought desperation – a cathartic episode created by my desire to find love in this loveless world?

Quite suddenly, as I stared at Mina, an idea occurred to me. I smiled at the thought.

She looked up. 'What is it?'

I said, 'I want to write a new novel, Mina.'

Her face clouded. 'About what happened?'

I stared at her beautiful left hand, resting upon her knee. 'No,' I said. 'It will be about you . . . If you'll let me, that is.'

She had always been reluctant to have me write about her, as if by doing so I might claim possession of the part of her that she had been so careful to withhold.

Now she smiled. 'I think perhaps I might,' she said.

This novel is dedicated with love to Mina, for showing me that the true measure of love is one's actions, not words.

Dedication in Daniel Ellis's novel *A Woman of Quality*.

'Ken MacLeod has the ability to bring about a seamless transition from the recognisably conventional *as is* to the most outrageous science fictional *what if?*, without appearing to break the creative equivalent of a sweat. *The Human Front* has pretty much everything you could ask from a great story: character, insight, plot, that quality of description that transports a feeling, sensation, incident or a landscape seemingly direct from world to mind, and revelation. It has substance. It should make your mind reel and work.'

Iain M. Banks

Also by Ken MacLeod:

The Web: Cydonia

KEN MACLEOD

The Human Front

The right of Ken MacLeod to be identified as the author
of this work has been asserted by him in accordance
with the Copyright, Designs and Patents Act 1988.

First published in Great Britain in 2002 by
Gollancz
An imprint of the Orion Publishing Group
Orion House, 5 Upper St Martin's Lane,
London WC2H 9EA

This edition published in Great Britain in 2003
by Gollancz

A CIP catalogue record for this book
is available from the British Library

ISBN 0 575 07505 8

Typeset at The Spartan Press Ltd,
Lymington, Hants

Printed in Great Britain by
Clays Ltd, St Ives plc

Like most people of my generation, I remember exactly where I was on March 17, 1963, the day Stalin died. I was in the waiting-room of my father's surgery, taking advantage of the absence of waiting patients to explore the nicotine-yellowed stacks of *Reader's Digest*s and *National Geographic*s, and to play in a desultory fashion with the gnawed plastic soldiers, broken tin tanks, legless dolls and so forth that formed a disconsolate heap, like an atrocity diorama, in one corner. My father must have been likewise taking advantage of a slack hour towards the end of the day to listen to the wireless. He opened the door so forcefully that I looked up, guiltily, though on this particular occasion I had nothing to be guilty about. His expression alarmed me further, until I realised that the mixed feelings that struggled for control of his features were not directed at me.

Except one. It was with, I now think, a full awareness of the historic significance of the moment, as well as a

1
·

certain sense of loss, that he told me the news. His voice cracked slightly, in a way I had not heard before.

'The Americans,' he said, 'have just announced that Stalin has been shot.'

'Up against a wall?' I asked, eagerly.

My father frowned at my levity and lit a cigarette.

'No,' he said. 'Some American soldiers surrounded his headquarters in the Caucasus mountains. After the partisans were almost wiped out they surrendered, but then Stalin made a run for it and the American soldiers shot him in the back.'

I almost giggled. Things like this happened in history books and adventure stories, not in real life.

'Does that mean the war is over?' I asked.

'That's a good question, John.' He looked at me with a sort of speculative respect. 'The Communists will be disheartened by Stalin's death, but they'll go on fighting, I'm afraid.'

At that moment there was a knock on the waiting-room door, and my father shooed me out while welcoming his patient in. The afternoon was clear and cold. I mucked about at the back of the house and then climbed up the hill behind it, sat on a boulder and watched the sky. A pair of eagles circled their eyrie on the higher hill opposite, but I didn't let that distract me. After a while my patience was rewarded by the thrilling sight of a V-formation of American bombers high above, flying east. Their circular shapes glinted

silver when the sunlight caught them, and shadowed black against the blue.

. . .

The newspapers always arrived on Lewis the day after they were printed, so two days passed before the big black headline of the *Daily Express* blared **STALIN SHOT**, and I could read, without fully comprehending, the rejoicing of Beaverbrook, the grave commentary of Cameron, the reminiscent remarks of Churchill, and frown over Burchett's curiously disheartening reports from the front, and smile over the savage raillery of Cummings' cartoon of Stalin in hell, shaking hands with Satan while hiding a knife behind his back.

Obituaries traced his life: from the Tiflis seminary, through the railway yards and oilfields of Baku, the bandit years as Koba, the October Revolution and the Five-Year Plans, the Purges and the Second World War; his chance absence from the Kremlin during the atomic bombing of Moscow in Operation Dropshot, and his return in old age to the ways and vigour of his youth as a guerrilla leader, rallying Russia's remaining Reds to the protracted war against the Petrograd government; to the contested, gruesome details of his death and the final, bloody touch, the fingerprint identification of his hacked-off hands.

By then I had already had a small aftershock of the revolutionary's death myself, at school on the 18th.

Hugh MacDonald, a pugnacious boy of nine or so but still in my class, came up to me in the playground and said: 'I bet you're pleased, *mac a dochter*.'

'Pleased about what?'

'About the Yanks killing Stalin, you *cac*.'

'And why should I not be? He was just a murderer.'

'He killed Germans.'

Hugh looked at me to see if this produced the expected change of mind, and when it didn't he thumped me. I kicked his shin and he ran off bawling, and I got the belt for fighting.

That evening I played about with the dial of my father's wireless, and heard through a howl of atmospherics a man with a posh Sassenach accent reading out eulogies on what the Reds still called Radio Moscow.

The genius and will of Stalin, great architect of the rising world of free humanity, will live forever.

I had no idea what it meant, or how anyone even remotely sane could possibly say it, but it remained in my mind, part of the same puzzle as that unexpected punch.

• • •

My father, Dr Malcolm Donald Matheson, was a native of the bleak long island. His parents were crofters who had worked hard and scraped by to support him in his medical studies at Glasgow in the 1930s. He had only

4
•

just graduated when the Second World War broke out. He volunteered for combat duty and was immediately assigned to the Royal Army Medical Corps. Of his war service, mainly in the Far East, he said very little in my hearing. It may have been some wish to pay back something to the community that had supported him which led him to take up his far from lucrative practice in the western parish of Uig, but of sentiment towards that community he had none. He insisted on being addressed by the English form of his name, instead of as 'Calum' and I and my siblings were likewise identified: John, James, Margaret, Mary, Alexander – any careless references to Iain, Hamish, Mairead, Mairi or Alasdair met a frown or a mild rebuke. Though a fluent native speaker of Gaelic, he spoke the language only when no other communication were possible – there were, in those days, a number of elderly monoglots, and a much larger number of people who never used the English language for any purpose other than the telling of deliberate lies. There are two explanations, one fanciful and the other realistic, for the latter phenomenon. The fanciful one is that they believed that the Gaelic was the language of heaven (was the Bible not written in it?) and that the Almighty did not hear, or did not understand, the English; or, at the very least, that a lie not told in Gaelic didn't count. The realistic one is that English was the language of the state, and lying in its hearing was indeed legitimate,

since the Gaels had heard so many lies from it, all in English.

My mother, Morag, was a Glaswegian of Highland extraction, who had met and married my father after the end of the Second World War and before the beginning of the Third. She, somewhat contrarily, taught herself the Gaelic and used it in all her dealings with the locals, though they always thought her dialect and her accent stuck-up and affected. The thought of her speaking a pure and correct Gaelic in a Glasgow accent is amusing; her neighbours' attitude towards her well-meant efforts less so, being an example of the characteristic Highland inferiority complex so often mistaken for class or national consciousness. The Lewis accent itself is one of the ugliest under heaven, a perpetual weary resentful whine – the Scottish equivalent of Cockney – and the dialect thickly corrupted with English words Gaelicised by the simple expedient of mispronouncing them in the aforementioned accent.

Before marriage she had been a laboratory assistant. After marriage she worked as my father's secretary, possibly for tax reasons, while raising me and my equally demanding brothers and sisters. Like my father, she was a smoker, a whisky-drinker, and an atheist. All of these were, at that time and place, considered quite inappropriate for a woman, but only the first was publicly known. Our non-attendance at any of the three doctrinally indistinguishable but mutually

irreconcilable churches the parish supported was explained by the rumour – perhaps arising from my father's humanitarian contribution to the war effort – that the *dochter* was a Quaker. It was a notion he did nothing to encourage or to dispel. The locals wouldn't have recognised a Quaker if they'd found one in their porridge.

Because of my father's military service and medical connections, he had stroll-in access at the nearby NATO base. This sprawling complex of low, flat-roofed buildings, Nissen huts, and radar arrays disfigured the otherwise sublime headland after which the neighbouring village, Aird, was named. My father occasionally dropped in for cheap goods – big round tins of cigarettes, packs of American nylons for my mother, stacks of chewing-gum for the children, and endless tins of corned beef – at the NAAFI store.

It was thus that I experienced the event which became the second politically significant memory of my childhood, and the only time when my father expressed a doubt about the Western cause. He was, I should explain, a dyed-in-the-wool conservative and unionist, hostile even to the watery socialism of the Labour Party, but he would have died sooner than vote for the Conservative and Unionist Party. 'The Tories took our land,' he once spat, by way of explanation, before slamming the door in the face of a rare, hopeless canvasser. He showed less emotion at Churchill's death

than he did at Stalin's. So, like most of our neighbours, he was a Liberal. The Liberals had, in their wishy-washy Liberal way, decried the Clearances, and the Highlanders have loyally returned them to Parliament ever since.

Why the Highlanders nurse a grievance over the Clearances was a mystery to me at the time, and still is. In no land in the world is the disproportion between natural attraction and sentimental attachment more extreme, except possibly Poland and Palestine. Expelled from their sodden Sinai to Canada and New Zealand the dispossessed crofters flourished, and those who remained behind had at last enough land to feed themselves, but their descendants still talk as if they'd been put on cattle trucks to Irkutsk.

It was my habit, when I had nothing better to do on a Saturday, to accompany my father on his rounds. I did not, of course, attend his consultations, but I would either wait in the car or brave the collies who'd press their forepaws on my shoulders and bark in my face, to the inevitable accompaniment of cries of 'Och, he's just being friendly,' and make my way through mud and cow-dung to the hospitality of black tea in the black houses, and the fussing of immense mothers girt in aprons and shod in wellingtons.

We'd visited an old man in Aird that morning in the summer of '63, and my father turned the Hillman off the main road and up to the NATO base. Gannets

dropped like dive-bombs in the choppy sea of the bay below the headland's cliffs, and black on the Atlantic horizon the radar turned. Though militarily significant – Lewis commands a wide sweep of the North Atlantic, and Tupolev's deep-shelter factories in the Urals were turning out long-range jet bombers at a rate of about one a month, well above attrition – security was light. A nod to the squaddie on the gate, and we were through.

My father casually pulled up in the officers' car-park outside the NAAFI and we hopped out. He was just locking the door when an alarm shrieked. Men in blue uniforms were suddenly rushing about and pointing out to sea. Other men, in white helmets and webbing, were running to greater purpose. Somewhere a fire-engine and an ambulance joined in the clamour.

I spotted the incoming bomber before my father did, maybe two miles out.

'There – there it is!'

'It's *low*—'

Barely above the sea, flashing reflected sunlight as it yawed and wobbled, trailing smoke, the bomber limped in. On the wide concrete apron in front of us a team frantically pushed and dragged a big Wessex helicopter to the perimeter, while one man stood waving what looked like outsize ping-pong bats. The bomber just cleared the top of the cliff, skimmed the grass – I could see the plants bend beneath it, though no blast of air came from it – and with a screaming

scrape and a shower of sparks it hit the concrete and slithered to a halt about a hundred yards from where we stood.

It was perhaps fifty feet in diameter, ten feet thick at the hub. Smoke poured from a ragged nick in its edge. The ambulance and fire-engine rushed up and stopped in a squeal of brakes, their crews leaping out just as a hatch opened on the bomber's upper side. More smoke puffed forth, but nothing else emerged. A couple of firemen, lugging fire-extinguishers, leapt on the sloping surface and dropped inside. Others hosed the rent in the hull.

My father ran forward, shouting 'I'm a doctor!' and I ran after him. The outstretched arm of one of the men in white helmets brought my father up short. After a moment of altercation, he was allowed to go on, while I struggled against a firm but not unfriendly grip on my shoulder. The man's armband read 'Military Police'. At that moment I was about ten yards from the bomber, close enough to see the rivets in its steel hull.

Close enough to see the body which the firemen lifted out, and which the ambulancemen laid on a stretcher and ran with, my father close behind, into the nearest building. It was wearing a close-fitting silvery flying-suit, and a visored helmet. One leg was crooked at a bad angle. That was not what shot me through with a thrill of horror. It was the body of a child, no taller than my five-year-old sister Margaret.

The large helmet made its proportions even more child-like.

A moment later I was turned around and hustled away. The military policeman almost pushed me back into the car, told me to wait there, and shut me up with a stick of chewing-gum before he hurried off. Everybody else who'd come at all close to the craft was being rounded up into a huddle guarded by the military policemen and being lectured by a couple of men who I guessed were civilians, if their snap-brimmed hats, dark glasses and black suits were anything to go by. They reminded me of American detectives in comics. I wondered excitedly if they carried guns in shoulder holsters.

After about fifteen minutes my father came out of the building and walked over to the car. One of the civilians intercepted him. They talked for a few minutes, leaning towards each other, their faces close together, one or other of them shaking their fingers, pointing and jabbing. Each of them glanced over at me several times. Although I had the side window wound down, I couldn't hear what they were saying. Eventually my father turned on his heel and stalked over to the car, while the other man stood looking after him. As my father opened the car door the black-suited civilian shook his head a little, then rejoined his colleague as the small crowd dispersed.

A knot of military policemen formed up at the

building's doorway, and surrounded two stretcher-bearers as they hurried to the Wessex. There was only the briefest glimpse of the stretcher as it was passed inside, moments before it took off and headed out to sea on a southerly course.

My father's face was pale and his hand shook as he took his hip-flask from the glove compartment. The top squeaked as he unscrewed it, the flask gurgled as he drank it dry.

'Leave the window down, John,' he said as he turned the key and pushed the starter. 'I need a cigarette.'

He lit up, fumbling, then engaged the gears and the car moved off with a lurch. As we passed the soldier on the gate my father gave him a wave that was almost a salute.

'What sort of people will that poor laddie be fighting for?' he asked me, or himself. His knuckles were white on the wheel. The swerve on to the main road threw me against the door. He didn't notice.

'Monsters,' he said. 'Monsters.'

I sat up straight again, rubbing my shoulder.

'It's awful to use wee children to fly bombers,' I said.

He looked across at me sharply, then turned his attention back to the single-track road.

'Is that what you saw?' he murmured. 'Well, John, we were told very firmly that the pilot was a midget, you know, a dwarf, and that this is a secret. If the enemy knew that, they would know something they

shouldn't know about our bombers. About how much weight they can carry, or something like that.'

I squirmed on the plastic leather, swinging my legs as though I needed to pee. I had read about dwarfs and midgets in *Look and Learn*. They were not like in fairy stories.

'But that's not true,' I said. 'That wasn't a dwarf, the pro— the portions—'

' "Proportions".'

'The proportions were wrong. I mean, they were right – they were ordinary. The pilot was a child, wasn't he?'

The car swerved slightly, then steadied.

'Listen, John,' my father said. 'Whatever the pilot is, neither of us is supposed to talk about it, and we'll get into big trouble if we do. So if you're sure it was a child you saw, I'm not going to argue with you. And if the Air Force say the pilot is a midget, I'm not going to argue with them, either. I set and splinted the leg of that, that' – he hesitated, waving a hand danger-ously off the wheel – '*craitur beag 'us bochd* – of the poor wee thing, I should say, and that's all I know of it.'

I was as startled by his lapse into the Gaelic as by the uncertainty and ambiguity of his reference to the pilot, and I thought it wise to keep quiet about the whole subject. But he didn't, not quite yet.

'Not a word about it, to anyone,' he said. 'Not to your

mother, your brothers and sisters, your friends, anyone. Not a word. Promise me?'

'All right,' I said. I was young enough to feel that it was more exciting to keep a secret than to tell one.

The following day was a Sunday, and although it meant nothing to us but a day off school we had to conform to local custom by not playing outside. It was a sweltering hell of boredom, relieved only by the breath of air from the open back door and the arrival at the front door of two men in black suits, who weren't ministers. My father escorted them politely into his surgery. The waiting-room door (I found, on a cautious test) was locked. They did not stay long; but the following morning on the way out to catch the van to school I overheard my mother telephoning around to postpone the day's appointments, and noticed a freshly emptied whisky bottle on the trash.

• • •

A couple of years later, when I was ten, my father sold his practice to a younger, less financially straitened and more idealistic doctor (a Nationalist, to my father's private disgust) and took up a practice in Greenock, an industrial town on the Firth of Clyde. Our flitting was exciting, our arrival more so. It was another world. In the mid-sixties the Clyde was booming, its shipyards producing naval and civilian vessels in almost equal proportion, its harbours crowded with British and

American warships, the Royal Ordnance Factory at Bishopton working around the clock. Greenock, as always, flourished from the employment opportunities upriver – beginning with the yards and docks of the adjacent town of Port Glasgow – and from its own industries, mainly the processing of colonial sugar, jute and tobacco. The pollution from the factories and refineries was light, but fumes from the heavy vehicular traffic that serviced them may well explain the high incidence of lung cancer in the area. (My father's death, though outside the purview of the present narrative, may also be so accounted.) Besides these traditional industries, a huge IBM factory had recently opened (the ceremonial ribbon cut by Sir Alan Turing himself) in the Kip Valley behind the town.

The town's division between middle class and working class was sharp. On the eastern side of Nelson Street lay the tenements and factories; to the west a classical grid of broad streets blocked out sturdy sandstone villas and semi-detached houses. Though our parents' disdain for private education saved us from the worst snobberies of fee-paying schools, the state system was just as blatantly segregated. The grammar schools filled the offices of management, and the secondary moderns manufactured workers. Class division shocked me: after growing up among the well-fed, if ill-clad, population of Lewis, I saw the poorer eight-tenths of the town as inhabited by misshapen dwarfs.

15

It was while exploring what to my imagination were dangerous, Dickensian slums, but which were in reality perfectly respectable working-class districts, that I first encountered evidence that this division was regarded, by some, as part of the greater division of the world. On walls, railway bridges and pavements I noticed a peculiar graffito, in the shape of an inverted 'Y' with a cross-bar – a childishly simple, and therefore instantly recognisable, representation of the human form. Sometimes it was enclosed by the outline of a five-pointed star, and frequently it was accompanied by a scrawled hammer and sickle. These last two symbols were, of course, already familiar to me from the red flags of the enemy.

It was at first as shocking a sight as if some Chinese or Russian guerrilla had popped out of a manhole in the street, and it gave me a strange thrill – a *frisson*, as the French say – to find that the remote and gigantic foe had his partisans in the streets of Greenock as much as in the jungles of Malaya or the rubble of Budapest. One day in 1966 I actually met one, on a street corner in the East End, down near the town centre where the big shops began.

This soldier of the Red horde was a bandy-legged old man in a cloth cap, selling copies of a broadsheet newspaper called the *Daily Worker*. He met with neither hostility nor interest from the passers-by. With boyish bravado, and some curiosity, I bought it. Its masthead

displayed the two symbols I already knew, and an article inside was illustrated by, and explained, the third.

'Against the warmongers and arms profiteers, against the reckless drive to destruction, against the forces of death, it is necessary to rally all who yearn for peace. The situation cries out for the broadest possible united front, one broader even than the great People's Fronts against fascism, one in which every decent human being, every worker, every woman, every honest businessman, every farmer, every patriot can take their place with pride and determination. It is not for any political party, or class, or ideology that such a front shall stand, but for the very survival of the human race.

'This greatest of all united and people's fronts exists, and is growing.

'It is the Human Front.'

I understood barely a word of it, and the only reason why I clipped out the article and kept it, long after I had secretly disposed of the newspaper, long enough for me to re-read and finally understand it, years later, was because of coincidental resonances of its author's name – Dr John Lewis.

· · ·

After that initial naive exploration I settled down to a sort of acceptance of the world as it was, and to learning more about it, at school and out. Science was more

interesting than politics, and it soothed rather than
disturbed the mind. The war was a permanent backdrop
of news, and a distant prospect of National Service. The
BBC brought it home on the wireless and, increasingly,
on black-and-white television, with feigned neutrality
and unacknowledged censorship. News items that
raised questions about the war's conduct and its domestic repercussions were few: the Pauling trial, the
Kinshasa atomic bombing, the occasional allusion to a
speech by Foot in the Commons or Wedgwood Benn in
the Lords.

The biggest jolt to the consensus came in 1968, with
the May Offensive. Out of nowhere, it seemed, the
supposedly defeated *maquis* stormed and seized Paris,
Lyons, Nantes, and scores of other French cities. Only
carpet-bombing of the suburbs dislodged them and
saved the Versailles government. This could not be
hidden, nor the first anti-war demonstrations in the
United States: clean-cut students chanting 'Hey! Hey!
JFK! How many kids did you kill today?' until the dogs
and fire-hoses and tear-gas cleared the streets. At the
time, I was more frightened by the unexpected close-
ness of the Communist threat than shocked by the
measures taken against it.

My first act of dissidence wasn't until three years
later, at the age of seventeen. I slipped out one April
evening to attend a meeting in the Co-operative Hall
held under the auspices of Medical Aid for Russia. The

speaker was touring the country, and it may have been the controversy that followed him that drew the crowd of a hundred or so. It's certainly what drew me. He was flanked on the platform by a local trade union official, a pacifist lady, and Greenock's perennially unsuccessful Liberal candidate. (The local Labour MP had, naturally, denounced the meeting in the *Greenock Telegraph*.) The hall was bare, decorated with a few union banners and a portrait of Keir Hardie. I sat near the back, recognising no one except the little old man who'd once sold me the *Daily Worker*.

After some dull maundering from the union official, the pacifist lady stood up and introduced the speaker, the Argentine physician Dr Ernesto Lynch. A black-haired, bearded man, about forty, asthmatic, charismatic, apologetic about his cigar-smoking and his English, he brought the audience to their feet and sent me home in a fury.

'You're too gullible,' my father said. 'It's all just Communist propaganda.'

'Hiroshima, Nagasaki, Moscow, Magnitogorsk, Dien Bien Phu, Belgrade, Kinshasa!' I pounded the names with my fist on my palm. 'They happened! Nobody *denies* they happened!'

He lidded his eyes and looked at me through a veil of cigarette smoke. Bare elbows on the kitchen table, mother in the next room, the hiss of water on the iron, the Third Programme concerto in the background.

'If you had seen what I saw in Burma,' he said mildly, 'you wouldn't be so sorry about Hiroshima and Nagasaki. And the men who went into the Vorkuta camps weren't sorry about Moscow, and—'

'And what troops "liberated" Siberia?' I raged. 'The dirty Japs! With their hands still bloody from Vladivostok! Their hands *and* their—'

I stopped myself just in time.

'Look, John,' he said. 'We could go on shouting at each other all night about which side's atrocities are worse. The very fact that we can, that this Argentine johnny can tour the country and half the bloody Empire with his tales of heroic partisans in the Ukraine and sob stories about butchered villagers in Byelorussia, while nobody from our side could possibly do anything remotely similar in the Red territories, shows which side has the least to fear from the truth.'

'Britain didn't let the Nazis speak here during the war – William Joyce was hanged—'

He poured another whisky, and offered me one. I accepted it, ungraciously.

'We listened to Lord Haw-Haw and Tokyo Rose for a *laugh*,' he was saying. 'Then they were decently hanged, or decently jailed.'

'Pity we're on the same side now,' I said. 'Maybe the Yanks should let Tokyo Rose *out*. "Ruthki soldjah, you know what ith happening to you girrfliend? Big niggah boyth ith giving her big niggah—'

Again, I shut up just in time.

'Your racial prejudices are showing, young man,' Malcolm said. 'I thought Reds were supposed to be against the colour bar.'

'Huh!' I snorted. 'I thought Liberals were!'

'The colour bar will come down in good time,' he said. 'When both whites and coloureds are ready for it. Meanwhile, the Reds will be happy to agitate against it, while out of the other side of their mouths they'll spout the most blatant racialism and national prejudice, just as it suits them – anything to divide the free world.'

'Some free world that includes the American South, South Africa, Spain, Japan, and the Fourth Reich! That holds on to Africa with atom bombs! That relies on the dirty work of Nazi scientists!'

He tapped a cigarette and looked at it meditatively.

'What do you mean by that?'

'The bombers. They're what's made the whole war possible, from Dropshot onwards, and it was the Germans who invented them – to finish what Hitler started!'

He lit up, and shook his head.

'Werner von Braun died a very disappointed man,' he said. 'Unlike the rocket scientists the Russians got. They got to see their infernal researches put to use all right, with dire consequences for our side – mostly civilian targets, I might add, since you seem so upset about bombing civilians. At least our bomber pilots risk

their own lives, unlike the Russian missilemen who deal out death from hundreds of miles away.'

I could see what he was doing, deflecting our moral dispute into a purely intellectual, historical debate, and I was having none of it.

'Yeah, I wonder if the Yanks are still sending *children* up to fly the bombers.'

He almost choked on his sip of whisky. Through the open door of the living-room came the sound of the iron crashing to the floor and my mother's shout of annoyance. A moment later she said, sharply: 'James! Margaret! Off to bed!' A faint protest, a scurry, a slam. She bustled through, hot in her pinny, and closed the door and sat down. Her flush paled in seconds. My father glanced at her and said nothing.

They both looked so frightened that I felt scared myself.

'What's— What did— ?'

My mother leaned forward and spoke quietly.

'Listen, Johnny,' she said. I bristled; she hadn't called me that for years. She sighed. 'John. You're old enough to do daft things. You could go off and join the Army tomorrow, or you could get married, and there's not a thing we could do about either. And it's the same with listening to Communists and repeating their rubbish. It's a free country. Ruin your prospects if you like. But there's one thing I ask you. Just one thing. Don't ever, *ever*, ever say anything about what you and your father

saw in Aird. Don't even drop a hint. Because if you do, you'll ruin us all.'

'You never said this to me before!'

'Never thought we had to,' Malcolm said gruffly. 'You kept your mouth shut when you were a wee boy, as you promised, and good for you, and I thought that maybe over the years you had forgotten all about it.'

'How could I forget that?' I said.

He shrugged one shoulder.

'All right, all right,' I said. 'But I don't understand why it's such a big secret. I mean, surely the age or is it the *size* of the—'

My father leaned across the table and put his hand across my mouth – not as a gesture, as a physical shutting up.

'Not one word,' he said.

I leaned back and made wiping movements.

'OK, OK,' I said. 'Leave that aside. What were we talking about before? Oh yes, you were saying it wasn't the Nazis who invented the flying disc. So who do you think did?'

'Who knows? The Allies had Einstein and Oppenheimer and Turing and a lot of other very clever chaps, and it's all classified anyway, so, as I said – who knows?'

'How do you know it *wasn't* the Germans, then?'

'They weren't working along those lines.'

'Oh, come on!' I said. 'I've seen pictures of the things from during the war.'

'These were experimental circular airframes with entirely conventional propulsion,' he said. 'That doesn't describe the bombers, now does it? Have you ever heard of Nazi research into anti-gravity?'

'Have you ever heard of American?'

He shook his head.

'It's all classified, of course. But it was obviously a bigger breakthrough than the atomic bomb. Consider the Manhattan Project, and all the theory that led up to it.' He paused, to let this sink in. 'What I'd like you to do, John, is to use your head as well as keep your mouth shut. By all means rattle off the standard lefty rant about Nazi scientists, but do bear in mind that you're talking nonsense.'

I was baffled. My mother was looking worried.

'But,' I said, 'the *Americans* say it was German scientists who developed it.'

'They do indeed, John, they do indeed.'

He looked quite jovial; I think he was a little bit drunk.

'I think you've said enough,' my mother told him.

'That I have,' he said. 'Or too much. And you too, John. You have homework to do tonight and school to go to tomorrow. Goodnight.'

· · ·

The following day I felt rather flat, whether as a result of the unaccustomed glass of whisky or my father's

successful deflection of my moral outrage. After school I walked straight to the public library. My parents never worried if I didn't come home from school directly, so long as I phoned if I wasn't going to be home for my tea.

The library was a big Georgian-style pile in the town centre. I stepped in and breathed the exhilarating smell of dark polished wood and of old and new paper. It took me only a minute to Dewey-decimal my way around the high stacks to the aviation section. Sheer nostalgia made me reach for the first in the row of tiny, well-worn editions of the *Observer's Book of Aircraft*. I still had that 1960 edition, somewhere at home. Flicking past the familiar silhouettes of Lancaster and Lincoln and MiG, I looked again at the simplest outline of the lot: the circular plan and lenticular profile of the Advanced High Altitude Bomber, Mark 1. The description and specifications were understandably sparse ('outperforms all other aircraft, Allied and enemy'), the history routine: first successful test flight, from White Sands to Roswell Army Air Field, New Mexico, July 1947; first combat use, Operation Dropshot, September 1949; extensive use in all theatres since.

I replaced the volume and pulled out the fresh 1970 edition, its cover colour photo of a Brabant still glossy. The AHAB's description, specs, and history were identical, and identically uninformative, but the designation had changed. Checking back a couple of volumes, I found that the AHAB-2 had come into service in 1964.

It didn't take me much longer to find that the biggest military innovation of the previous year had been the Russian MiG-24, capable of reaching a much higher altitude than its predecessors. I sought traces of the AHAB in more detailed works, one of which stated that none had ever been shot down over enemy territory. All of that got me thinking, but what struck me even more was that after more than twenty years there wasn't a dicky-bird about the machine's development, beyond the obviously (now that it was pointed out) misleading references to wartime German experimental aircraft. Nor were there any civilian or wider military applications of the revolutionary physical principles behind its anti-gravity engine.

I tried looking up anti-gravity in other stacks: physics, military history, biography. Beyond the obvious fact that it was used in the AHAB, there was nothing. No speculation. No theory. No big names. No obscure names. Nothing. Fuck all.

I walked home with a heavy load of books and a head full of anti-gravity.

· · ·

'Outer space,' said Ian Boyd, confidently. Four or five of us were sitting out a free period on our blazers on damp grass on the slope of the hill above the playing-field. Below us the fourth-year girls were playing hockey. Now and again a run or swerve would lift the skirt of

one of them above her knees. We were here for these moments, and for the more reliable sight of their breasts pushing out their crisp white shirts.

'What d'ye mean, outer space?' asked Daniel Orr.

'Where they came frae. The flying discs.'

'Oh aye. Dan Dare stuff.'

'Don't you Dan Dare me, Dan Orr.'

This variant on a then-popular catch-phrase had us all laughing.

'We know there's life out there,' Ian persisted. 'Astronomers say there's at least lichens on Mars, they can see the vegetation spreading up frae the equator every year. An it's no that far-fetched there's life on Venus an a', underneath the cloud cover.'

'No evidence of intelligent life, though,' Daniel said.

'No up there,' said Colin NcNicol. 'There is down there.'

'Aye, there's life, but is it intelligent?'

We all laughed and concentrated for a while on the hockey-playing aliens, with their strange bodies and high-pitched cries.

'It's intelligent,' said Ian. 'The problem is, how dae we communicate?'

'No, the *first* problem is, how do we let them know we're friendly?'

'Tell them we come in peace.'

'And we want to come inside.'

'*If*,' I said, mercilessly mimicking our Classics teacher,

27

'you gentlemen are quite ready to return the conversation to serious matters—'

'This is serious a' right!'

'Future ae the entire human race!'

'Patience, gentlemen, patience. Withhold your ejaculations. Your curiosity on these questions will be soon be fully satisfied. The annual lecture on "Human Reproduction In One Minute" will be prematurely presented to the boys later this year by Mr Hughes, in his class on Anatomy, Physiology, and Stealth. The girls will simultaneously and separately receive a lecture on "Human Reproduction In Nine Months" as part of their Domestic Science course. Boys and girls are not allowed to compare notes until after marriage, or pregnancy, whichever comes sooner. Meanwhile, I understand that Professor Boyd here has a point to make.'

'Oh aye, well, if it wisni the Yanks an' it wisni the Jerries, it must hae come frae somewhere else—'

'The annual prize for Logic—'

'—so it must hae been the Martians.'

'—has just been spectacularly lost at the last moment by Professor Boyd, after a serious objection from Brother William of Ockham—'

'Hey, nae papes in our school!'

'—who presents him, instead, with the conical paper cap inscribed in memory of Duns Scotus, for the *non sequitur* of the year.'

• • •

Near the High School was a park with a couple of reservoirs. Around the lower of them ran a rough path, and its circumambulation was a customary means of working off the stodge of school dinner. A day or two after our frivolous conversation, I was doing this unaccompanied when I heard a hurrying step behind me, and turned to see Dan Orr catch me up. He was a slim, dark, intense youth who, though a month or two younger than me, had always seemed more mature. The growth of his limbs, unlike mine, had remained proportionate, and their movements under the control of the motor centres of his brain. His father was, I believe, an engineer at the Thompson yard.

'Hi, Matheson.'

'Greetings, Orr.'

'Whit ye were saying the other day.'

'About the bombers?'

'Naw.' He waved a hand. 'That's no an issue. We'll never find out, anyway, and between you an me I couldni give a flying fuck if they were invented by Hitler himsel, or the Mekon of Mekonta fir that matter.'

'That's a point of view, I suppose.' We laughed. 'So what is the issue?'

'Come on, Matheson, ye know fine well whit the issue is. It isnae where they *came* frae. It's where they *go*, and whit they *dae* to folk.'

'Aye,' I said cautiously.

'Ye were at that meeting, right?'

'How would you know if I was?'

'Yir face is as red as yir hair, ya big teuchter. But not as red as Willie Scott of the AEU, who was on the platform and gave a very full account o the whole thing tae his Party branch.'

'Good God!' I looked sideways at him, genuinely astonished. 'You're in the CP?'

'No,' he said. 'The Human Front.'

'Well kept secret,' I said.

He laughed. 'It's no a secret. I just keep my mouth shut at school for the sake o the old man.'

'Does he know about it?'

'Oh, aye, sure. He's Labour, but kindae a left winger. Anyway, Matheson, what did you think about what Dr Lynch had tae say?'

I told him.

'Well, fine,' he said. 'The question is, d'ye want tae dae something about it?'

'I've already put my name down to raise money for Medical Aid.'

'That's good,' he said. 'But it's no enough.'

We negotiated an awkward corner of the path, leaping a crumbled culvert. Orr ended up ahead of me.

'Dr Lynch,' he said over his shoulder, 'had some other things tae say, about what people can do. And we're discussing them tonight.' He named a café. 'Back room, eight sharp. Drop by if ye like. Up tae you.'

He ran on, leaving me to think.

. . .

Heaven knows what Orr was thinking of, inviting me to that meeting. The only hypothesis which makes sense is that he had shrewdly observed me over the years of our acquaintance, and knew me to be reliable. I need not describe the discussion here. Suffice it to say that it was in response to a document written by Lin Piao which Dr Lynch had clandestinely distributed during his tour, and which was later published in full as an appendix to various trial records. I was not aware of that at the time, and the actual matters discussed were of a quite elementary, and almost entirely legal, character, quite in keeping with the broad nature of the Front. It was only later that I was introduced to the harsher regimens in Dr Lynch's prescription.

We started small. Over the next few weeks, what time I could spare from studying for my Highers, in evenings, early mornings, and weekends, was taken up with covering the town's East End and most of Port Glasgow with the slogans and symbols of the Front, as well as some creative interpretations of our own.

FREE DUBCEK, we wrote on the walls of the Port Glasgow Municipal Cleansing works, in solidarity with a then-famous Czechoslovak guerrilla leader being held incommunicado by NATO. To the best of my

knowledge it is still there, though time has worn the 'B' to a 'P'.

And, our greatest coup, on the enormous wall of the Thompson yard, in blazing white letters and tenacious paint that no amount of scrubbing could entirely erase:

FORGET KING BILLY AND THE POPE

UNCLE JOE'S OUR ONLY HOPE

The Saturday after the last of my Higher exams, I happened to be in the car with my father, returning from a predictably disastrous Morton match at Cappie-low, when we passed that slogan. He laughed.

'I must say I agree with the first line,' he said. 'The second line, well, it takes me back. Good old Uncle Joe, eh? I must admit I left "Joe for King" on a few shit-house walls myself. Amazing that people still have faith in the old butcher.'

'But is it really?' I said. I told him of my long-ago (it seemed – seven years, my God!) playground scrap over the memory of Stalin.

'It's fair enough that he killed Germans,' Malcolm said. 'Or even that he killed Americans. The problem some people, you know, have with Stalin is that he killed *Russians*, in large numbers.'

'It was a necessary measure to prevent a counter-revolution,' I said stiffly.

Malcolm guffawed. 'Is that what they're teaching you these days? Well, well. What would have happened in

the SU in the 30s if there had been a counter-revolution?'

'It would have been an absolute bloody massacre,' I said hotly. 'Especially of the Communists, and let's face it, they were the most energetic and educated people at the time. They'd have been slaughtered.'

'Damn right,' said Malcolm. 'So we'd expect – oh, let me see, most of the Red Army's generals shot? Entire cohorts of the Central Committee and the Politburo wiped out? Countless thousands of Communists killed, hundreds of thousands sent to concentration camps, along with millions of ordinary citizens? Honest and competent socialist managers and engineers and planners driven from their posts? The economy thrown into chaos by the turncoats and time-servers who replaced them? A brutal labour code imposed on the factory workers? Peasants rack-rented mercilessly? A warm handshake for Hitler? Vast tracts of the country abandoned to the fascist hordes? That the sort of thing you have in mind? That's what a counter-revolution would have been like, yes?'

'Something like that,' I said.

'That's exactly what happened, you dunderheid! Every last bit of it! Under Stalin!'

'How do we know that's not just propaganda from our side?'

'Here we go again,' he sighed. 'It's like arguing with a Free Presbyterian minister.'

'Come on,' I said. 'We know that a lot of what we're told in the press is lies. Look at the rubbish they were writing about how France was pacified, right up until the May Offensive! Look at—'

'Yes, yes,' he said. He pulled the car to a halt in the comfortable avenue where we lived, up by the golf course. He leaned back in his seat, took off his driving gloves and lit a cigarette.

'Look, John, let's not take this argument inside. It upsets your mother.'

'All right,' I said.

'You were saying about the press. Yes, it's quite true that a lot of lies are told about the war. I'll readily admit that, however much I still think the war is just. It was the same in the war with Hitler. Only to be expected. Censorship, misguided patriotism, wishful thinking – truth is the first casualty, and all that. So tell me this – who, in this country, has done the most to expose these lies?'

'Russell, I guess,' I said. After that I could only think of exiles and refugees from the ravaged Continent. 'And there's Sartre, and Camus, and Deutscher—'

'That's the man,' he said. 'Deutscher. Staunch Marxist. Former Communist. Respected alike by the *Daily Worker* and the *Daily Telegraph*. Man of the Left, man of integrity, right?'

'Yes,' I said, suspecting that he was setting me up for another fall. He was. When we went inside he

handed me a worn volume from his study's bowed bookshelves.

Deutscher's *Stalin*, published in 1948, was a complete eye-opener to me. I had never before encountered criticism of Stalin or his regime from the Left, nor so measured a judgement and matchless a style. It seemed to come from a vanished world, the world before Drop-shot, before the Fall.

. . .

'Fuck that,' said Dan Orr. 'Deutscher's a Trotskyite, for all that he's all right on the war. And Trotskyites are *scum*. I don't give a fuck how many o them Stalin killed. He didnae kill *enough*. There were still some alive tae be ministers in the Petrograd puppet government, alang wi all the Nazis and Ukrainian nationalists and NTS trash that the Yanks scraped out o the camps where they belonged.'

I didn't have an answer to that, at the time, so I shelved the matter. In any case we had more urgent decisions to make. Although we had not had our results yet, we both knew we had done well in our Highers, and could have gone straight to University the follow-ing September. This would have deferred our National Service until after graduation. Graduates could sign up for officer training. Most of our similarly successful classmates rejoiced at the opportunity to avoid the worst of the hardships and risks. Orr was adamant that

we should not take it. It was a principle with him (and with the Front, and with the Young Communist League of which, unknown to me at the time, he was a clandestine member).

'It's a blatant class privilege,' he said. 'Every working-class laddie has tae go as soon as he turns eighteen. Why should we be allowed tae dodge the column for four mair years? What gies us the right tae a cushy number? And think about it – when we've done our stint that'll be it over, we can get on wi university wi none o that growing worry about what's at the end o it, and in the meantime we'll hae learned to use a rifle and we can look every young worker in the eye, because we'll hae been through the same shit as he has.'

'But,' I said, 'suppose we find ourselves shooting at the freedom fighters?'

Or shot by them, was what was really worrying me.

'Cannae be helped,' said Orr. He laughed. 'I'm told it seldom comes tae that anyway. It's no like in the comics.'

My mother objected, my father took a more fatalistic approach. There was a scene, but I got my way.

We spent the summer working to earn some spending money and hopefully put some by in our National Savings Accounts. In the permanent war economy it was easy enough to walk into a job. Orr, ironically enough, became a hospital porter for a couple of

months, while I became a general labourer in the Thompson yard. We joked that we were working for each other's fathers.

The shipyard astounded me, in its gargantuan scale, its danger and din, and its peculiar combination of urgent pace and trivial delay. The unions were strong, management was complacent, work practices were restrictive and work processes were primitive. Parts of it looked like an Arab *souk*, with scores of men tapping copper pipes and sheets with little hammers over braziers. My accent had me marked instantly as a teuchter, a Highlander, which though humiliating was at least better than being written off as middle class. The older men had difficulty understanding me – I thought at first that this was an accent or language problem, and tried to conform to the Clydeside usage to ridiculous effect, until I realised that they were in fact partially deaf and I took to shouting in Standard English, like an ignorant tourist.

The Party branch at the yard must have known I was in the Front, but made no effort to approach me: I think there was a policy, at the time, of keeping students and workers out of each other's way. This backfired rather because it enabled me to encounter my first real live Trotskyist, who rather disappointingly was a second-year student working there for the summer. We had a lot of arguments. I have nothing more to say about that.

Most days after work I'd catch the bus to Nelson

Street, slog up through the West End to our house, have a bath and sleep for half an hour before a late tea. If I had any energy left I would go out, ostensibly for a pint or two but more usually for activity for the Front. The next stage in its escalating campaign, after having begun to make its presence both felt and over-estimated, was to discourage collaboration. This included all forms of fraternisation with American service personnel.

Port Glasgow is to the east of Greenock, Gourock to the west. The latter town combines a douce middle-class residential area and a louche seafront playground. Its biggest dance-hall, the Cragburn, a landmark piece of 30s architecture with a famously spring-loaded dance floor, draws people from miles around.

Orr and I met in the Ashton Café one Friday night in July. Best suits, Brylcreemed hair; scarves in our pockets. Hip-flask swig and gasper puff on the way along the front. The Firth was in one of its Mediterranean moments, gay-spotted with yachts and dinghies, grey-speckled with warships. Pound notes at the door. A popular beat combo, then a swing band.

We chose our target carefully, and followed her at distance after the dance. Long black hair down her back. She kissed her American sailor goodbye at the pier, waved to him as the liberty-boat pulled away. We caught up with her at a dark stretch of Shore Street, in the vinegar smell of chip-shops. Scarves over our noses

and mouths, my hand over her mouth. Bundled her into an alley, up against the wall. We didn't need the masks, not really. She couldn't look away from Orr's open razor.

'Listen, slag,' he said. 'Youse are no tae go out wi anybody but yir ain folk frae now on. Get it? Otherwise we'll cut ye.'

Tears glittered on her thick mascara. She attempted a nod.

'Something tae remind ye,' Orr said. 'And tae explain tae yir friends.'

He clutched her hair and cut it off with the razor, as close to the scalp as he could get. He threw the glistening hank at her feet and we ran before she could get out her first sob.

I threw up on the way home.

Three days later I overheard two lassies at the bus-stop. They were discussing the incident, or one like it. There had been several such, over the weekend, all the work of the Front.

'Looks like you're in deid trouble fae now on,' one of them concluded, 'if ye go out wi coons.'

• • •

Call-up papers arrived in August, an unwelcome 18th-birthday present. After nine weeks' basic training I was sent to Northern Ireland, where I spent the rest of my two-year stint guarding barracks, munitions dumps

and coastal installations. Belfast, Londonderry, south
Armagh: the most peaceful and friendly parts of the
British Empire.

Orr was sent to Rhodesia. His grave is in the Imperial
War Cemetery in Salisbury.

I was demobilised in September 1974, and went to
Glasgow University. My fellow first-year students were
all two years younger than me, including those in the
Front. The Party line had changed. Young men were
being urged to resist the war, to refuse conscription, to
take any deferral available, to burn their call-up papers
if necessary, to fill the jails. This was not because
the Party had become pacifist. It was because the Party,
and the Front, now had enough men with military
experience for the next step up Lin Piao's ladder.

People's War.

. . .

It is necessary to understand the situation at the time.
By 1974 the United States, Britain and the white
Dominions, Germany, Spain, Portugal and Belgium
were almost the only countries in the world without
a raging guerrilla war. Although nominally on the
Allied side, the governments of France and Italy were
paralysed, large tracts of both countries ungovernable
or already governed by the Resistance movements.
Every colony had its armed independence movement,
and every former socialist country had its re-liberated

territory and provisional government, even if driven literally underground by round-the-clock bombing.

'The peoples of the anti-imperialist camp long for peace every day,' wrote Lin Piao. 'Why do the peoples of the imperialist camp not long for peace? Unfortunately it is because they have no idea of what horrors are being suffered by the majority of the peoples of the world. It is necessary to bring the real state of affairs sharply to their attention. In order for the masses to irresistibly demand that the troops be brought home, it is necessary for the people's vanguard to bring home the war.'

. . .

That later came to be called the Lin Piao 'Left' Deviation. At the time it was called the line. I swallowed it whole.

I lodged in a bed-sitting-room in Glasgow, near the University, and took my laundry home at weekends. During my National Service I had only been able to visit occasionally, and had followed the Front's advice to keep my head down and my mouth shut about politics, on duty or off. It was a habit that I found agreeable, and I kept it. My parents assumed that my National Service had knocked all that nonsense out of me.

Greenock had changed. The younger and tougher and more numerous successors of the likes of Orr and me had shifted their attacks from the sailors'

girlfriends to the sailors, and the soldiers. They never attacked British servicemen, or even the police. At least a dozen Americans had been fatally stabbed, and two shot. Relations between the Americans and the town's population, hitherto friendly, had become characterised by suspicion on one side and resentment on the other. The cycle was self-reinforcing. Before long Americans were being attacked in quite non-political brawls, and off-duty Marines were picking fights with surly teenagers. The teenagers' angry parents would seek revenge. Other relatives would be drawn in. Before long an American serviceman couldn't be sure that any sweet-looking lass or little old lady wasn't an enemy.

Armed shore patrols in jeeps became a much more common sight. In the tougher areas, kids would throw stones at them. None of this was covered in the national press, and the *Greenock Telegraph* buried such accounts in brief reports of the proceedings of the Sheriff Court, but the *Daily Worker* reported similar events around US bases right across Britain.

I did not get involved in them. The first petrol-bombing, in January 1975, happened when I was in Glasgow. The first return fire from a group of US naval officers trapped in a stalled and surrounded staff car on the coast road – they'd started going further afield, to the quieter, smaller resort of Largs – took place in February, also mid-week, when I was definitely not in

Greenock. I read a brief report of it in the *Glasgow Herald*.

What was going on in Glasgow was political stuff, anti-war agitation, leafleting and picketing, that sort of thing. We took a hundred people from Glasgow to the big autumn demo in London. A hundred thousand or so converged on Grosvenor Square, with a militant contingent of ten thousand people chanting 'We shall fight! We shall win!' (we all agreed on that) and the Front's hotheads following it up with 'Joe! Joe! Joe Sta-lin!' or 'Long live Chairman Lin!' and the Trots trying to drown us out with a roar of 'London! Paris! Rome! Berlin!'

It was fun. I was serious. I knuckled down to the study of chemistry and physics (at Glasgow they still called the latter 'Natural Philosophy') which had always fascinated me. The Officer Training Corps would have been a risky proposition for me – even my very limited public political activity would have exposed me to endless hassles and security checks – but I joined the University's rifle club, which shared a shooting range and an armoury with the OTC. And I was still, of course, in the Reserves. Following the Front's advice, I kept out of trouble and bided my time.

. . .

I had seen the diagram a hundred times, and its physical manifestation, the iron filings forming furry

field-lines on a sheet of paper with a magnet under it, in my first-year physics class at High School. I had balanced magnets on top of each other, my fingers preventing them from flicking around and clicking together, and had felt the uncanny invisible spring pushing them apart. It was late one night in February 1975 when I was alone in my room, propping my head over an open physics textbook, that I first connected that sensation with my childhood chance observation of the curiously unstable motion or an anti-gravity bomber close to the ground, and with the magnetic field lines.

Was it possible, I wondered, that anti-gravity was a polar opposite of gravity, that keeping it stable was like balancing two magnets one upon the other, and that the field generated by the ship had the same shape as that of a magnet? If so, any missile approaching an AHAB bomber from above or below would be deflected, whereas one directed precisely at its edge, where the two poles of the field balanced, might well get through. The crippled bomber I'd seen had taken a hit edge-on, if that distant memory was reliable. The chance of that happening accidentally, even in a long war, might be slim enough for it to have happened only once. Yet the consequences of doing it deliberately were so awesome that this very possibility might well be the secret which the dark-suited security men had been so anxious to maintain. It seemed much more significant than the

minor, if grim, detail that the pilots were children or dwarfs.

It was an interesting thought, and I considered whether it might be possible to pass it upward through the Front and thence across to the revolutionary air forces. Come to think of it, to pass on all I knew, and all I'd seen at Aird. The thought made me shiver. I could not get away from the idea, so firmly instilled by my parents, that anything I might say along those lines would be traced back to me, and to them.

The Allied states, and Britain in particular, had at the time a sharp discontinuity in tolerance – their liberal and democratic self-definition almost forced them to put up with radical opposition, and to treat violent opposition as civil disorder rather than treason; while at the same time the necessities of the long war inclined them to totalitarian methods of maintaining military and state secrecy. A Front supporter could preach defeatism openly, and would receive at the worst police harassment and mob violence. A spy, or anyone under suspicion of materially aiding the enemy, would disappear and never be heard of again, or be summarily tried and executed. Rumours of torture cells and concentration camps proliferated. To what extent these were true was hard to judge, but irrelevant to their effect.

So I kept my theory to myself, and sought confirmation or refutation of it in war memoirs. Most from

the Red side were stilted and turgid. Those from former Allied soldiers were usually better written, even if sensationalised. If these accounts were reliable at all, the AHAB bombers were occasionally used for close air support and even medevac, in situations where (as my careful cross-checking made clear) there was little actual fighting in the vicinity and the weather was too violent for helicopters or other conventional aircraft.

I put my ideas about that on the back burner and got on with my work, until the Front had work for me. I left my studies without regret. It was like another call-up, and another calling.

· · ·

Davey stopped screaming when the morphine jab kicked in. Blood was still soaking from his trouser-leg all over the back seat of the stolen getaway car. He'd taken a high-velocity bullet just below the knee. What-ever was holding his shin on, it wasn't bone. In the yellow back-street sodium light all our faces looked sick and strange, but his was white. He sprawled, head and trunk in the rear footwell, legs on the back seat. I crouched beside him, holding the tourniquet, only slowing down the blood loss.

Andy, in the driver's seat, looked back over his shoulder.

'Take him tae the hospital?'

It was just up the road – we were parked, engine

idling, in a back lane by the sugarhouse. The molasses smell was heavy, the fog damp and smoky.

'We could dump him and run,' Gordon added pointedly, looking out and not looking back.

Save his leg and maybe his life for prison or an internment camp. No chance. But the Front's clandestine field hospitals were already overloaded tonight – we knew that from the news on the car radio alone.

'West End,' I said. 'Top of South Street.'

Andy slid the car into gear and we slewed the corner, drove up past the hospital and the West Station and around the roundabout at a legal speed that had me seething, even though I knew it was necessary. No Army patrols in this part of town, but there was no point in getting pulled by the cops for a traffic offence.

We stopped in a dark spot around the corner from my parents' house. Andy drove off to dump the car and Gordon and I lugged Davey through a door in a wall, past the backs of a couple of gardens, over a fence and into the back porch. I still had the keys. It had been two years since I'd last used them.

Balaclava off, rifle left behind the doorway, into the kitchen, light on. Somebody was already moving upstairs. I heard the sound of a shotgun breech closing.

'Malcolm!' I shouted, past the living-room door. 'It's just me!'

He made some soothing sounds, then said something firmer, and padded downstairs and appeared in the

living-room doorway, still knotting his dressing-gown. His face looked drawn in pencil, all grey lines. Charcoal shadows under the eyes. He started towards me.

'You're hurt!'

'It's not my blood,' I said.

His mouth thinned. 'I see,' he said. 'Bring him in. Kitchen floor.'

Gordon and I laid Davey out on the tiles, under the single fluorescent tube. The venetian blind in the window was already closed. My father reappeared, with his black bag. He washed his hands at the sink, stepped aside.

'Kettle,' he said.

I filled it and switched it on. He was scissoring the trouser-leg.

'Jesus Christ,' he said. 'Get this man to a hospital. I'm not a surgeon.'

'No can do,' I said. 'Do what you can.'

'I can stop him going into shock, and I can clean up and bandage.' He looked up at me. 'Top left cupboard. Saline bag, tube, needle.'

I held the saline drip while he inserted the needle. The kettle boiled. He sterilised a scalpel and forceps, tore open a bag of sterile swabs, and got to work quickly. After about five minutes he had Davey's wound cleaned and bandaged, the damaged leg splinted and both legs up on cushions on the floor. A dose of straight heroin topped up the morphine.

'Right,' Malcolm said. 'He'll live. If you want to save the leg, he must get to surgery right away.' He glared at us. 'Don't you bastards have field hospitals?'

'Overloaded,' I said.

His nose wrinkled. 'Busy night, huh?'

Davey was coming to.

'Take me in,' he said. 'I'll no talk.'

My father looked down at him.

'You'll talk,' he said; then, after a deep breath that pained him somehow: 'But I won't. I'll take him to the Royal, swear I saw him caught in crossfire.' He looked out at the rifles in the back porch, and frowned at me. 'Any powder on him?'

I shook my head, miserably.

'We didn't even get a shot in ourselves.'

'Too bad,' he said dryly. 'Right, you come with me, and you, mister,' he told Gordon, 'get yourself and your guns out of here before I see you, or them.'

Gordon glanced at me. I nodded.

'Through the cemetery,' I said.

I only just remembered to remove the revolver from Davey's jacket pocket. My mother suddenly appeared, gave me a tearful but silent hug, and started mopping the floor.

We straightened out a story on the way down, and I disappeared out of the car while my father went inside and got a couple of orderlies out with a stretcher. Ambulances came and went, sirens blaring, lights flashing. A

lot of uniforms about. By this time we were fighting the Brits as well as the Yanks. After a few minutes Malcolm returned, and I stepped out of the shadows and slid into the car.

'They bought it,' he said. He lit a cigarette and coughed horribly. 'Back to the house for a minute? Talk to your mother?'

'Dangerous for us all,' I said. 'If you could drop me off up at Barr's Cottage, I'd appreciate it. Otherwise, I'll hop out now.'

'I'll take you.'

Past the station again, at a more sedate pace.

'Thank you,' I said, belatedly. 'For everything.'

He grinned, keeping his eye on the road. ' "First, do no harm",' he said. 'Sort of thing.'

He drove in silence for a minute, around the round-about and out along Inverkip Road. The walls and high trees of the cemetery passed on the right. Gordon was probably picking his way through the middle of it by now.

'I'll give her your love,' he said. 'Yes?'

'Yes,' I said.

'Won't be seeing you again for another couple of years?'

'If that,' I answered, bleakly if honestly.

He turned off short of Barr's Cottage, into a council estate, and pulled in, under a broken streetlamp. The glow from another cigarette lit his face.

'All right,' he said. 'I have something to tell you.'

Another sigh, another bout of coughing.

'You may not see me again. Your mother doesn't know this yet, but I've got six months. If that.'

'Oh, God,' I said.

'Cancer of the lung,' he said. 'Lot of it about. Filthy air around here.' He crushed out the cigarette. 'Stick to rural guerrilla warfare in future, old chap. It's healthier than the urban variety.'

'I'll fight where I'm—'

His face blurred. I sobbed on his shoulder.

'Enough,' he said. He held me away, gently.

'There's no pain,' he assured me. 'Whisky, tobacco, and heroin, three great blessings. And as the Greek said, nothing is terrible when you know that being nothing is not terrible. I'll know when to ease myself out.'

'Oh, God,' I said again, very inaptly.

His yellow teeth glinted. 'I have no worries about meeting my maker. But, ah, I do have something on my conscience. A monkey on my back, which I want to offload on yours.'

'All right,' I said.

He leaned back and closed his eyes.

'Another time I treated a leg with a very similar injury . . .' he said. 'You were there then, too. You were much smaller, and so was the patient. You do remember?'

'Of course,' I said. My knees were shaking.

His eyes opened and he stared out through the wind-screen.

'The last time we discussed this,' he said, 'I suggested that you look into the origin of the bomber. No doubt you have read some books, given the matter thought, and drawn your own conclusions.'

'Yes,' I said, 'I certainly have, it's a—'

He held up one hand. 'Keep it,' he said. 'I've had a lot longer to think about the origin of the pilot. My first thought was the same as yours, that it was a child. Then, when I got, ah, a closer look, I must confess that my second thought was that I was seeing the work of . . . another Mengele. The grey skin, the four digits on hands and feet, the huge eyes, the coppery colour of the blood . . . I thought for years that this was the result of some perverted Nazi science, you know. But, like you, I've read a great deal since. And as a medical man, I know what can and can't be done. No rare syndrome, no surgery, no mutation, no foul tinkering with the germ-plasm could have made that body. It was not a deformed human body. It was a perfectly healthy, normal body, but it was not human.'

He turned to me, shaking his head. 'The memory plays tricks, of course. But in retrospect, and even taking that into account, I believe that the pilot was not only not human, but not mammalian. I'm not even sure that he was a *vertebrate*. The bones in the leg were—'

His cheek twitched. 'Like broken plastic, and hollow. Thin-walled, and filled with rigid tubes and struts rather than spongy bone and marrow.'

I felt like giggling.

'You're saying the pilot was from *another planet*?'

'No,' he said, sharply. 'I'm not. I'm telling you what I *saw*.' He waved a hand, his cigarette tip tracing a jiggly red line. 'For all I know, the pilot may be a specimen of some race of intelligent beings that evolved on Earth and lurks unseen in the depths of the fucking Congo, or the Himalayas, like the Abominable Snowman!'

He laughed, setting off another wheezing cough.

'So there it is, John. A secret I won't be taking to the grave.'

We talked a bit more, and then I got out of the car and watched the tail-lights disappear around a corner.

. . .

Scotland is not a good country for rural guerrilla warfare, having been long since stripped of trees and peasants. Without physical or social shelter, any guerrilla band in the hills and glens would be easily spotted and picked off, if they hadn't starved first. The great spaces of the Highlands were militarily irrelevant anyway.

So everybody believed, until the guerrilla war. Night,

clouds and rain, gullies, boulders, bracken, isolated clumps of trees, the few real forests, burns and bridges and bothies all provided cover. The relatively sparse population could do little to betray us and – voluntarily or otherwise – much to help, and supplied few targets for enemy reprisals against civilians. Deer, sheep and rabbits abounded, edible wild plants and berries grew everywhere, and vegetables were easily enough bought or stolen. The strategic importance of the coastline and the offshore oilfields, and the vulnerability and propaganda value of the larger towns – Fort William, Inverness, Aberdeen, Thurso – compelled the state's armed forces to hold the entire enormous area: to move troops and armour along the long, narrow moorland roads, through glens ideal for ambush, and to fly low over often-clouded hills; to guard hydroelectric power stations, railways, microwave relay masts, the military's own installations and training-grounds; to patrol hundreds of miles of pipelines and cables.

That was just the Highlands: the area where I was, for obvious reasons, sent. Those who fought in the Borders, the Pentlands, the Southwest, and even the rich farmland of Perthshire all discovered other options, other opportunities. And that is to say nothing of what the English and Welsh comrades were doing. By 1981 the Front was making the country burn. The line had changed – Deng Hsiao-Ping was making cautious advances in the Versailles negotiations – but the fighting

continued and we felt proud that we had fulfilled the late Chairman's directive. We had brought home the war.

• • •

The Bren was heavy and the pack was heavier. I was almost grateful that I had to move slowly. Moving under cloud cover was frustrating and dangerous. Visibility that October morning was a couple of metres; the clouds were down to about a hundred, and there was a storm on the way. Behind me nine men followed in line, down from the ridge. I found the bed of a burn, just a trickle at that moment, its boulders and pebbles slick and slippery from the rain of a week earlier. We made our way down this treacherous stairway from the invisible skyline we'd crossed. The first *glomach* I slipped into soaked me to the thighs.

I waded out and moved on. My ankle would have hurt if it hadn't been so cold. The light brightened and quite suddenly I was below the cloud layer, looking down at the road and the railway line at the bottom of the glen, and off to my right and to the west, a patch of meadow on the edge of a small loch with a crannog in the middle. Three houses, all widely separated, were visible up and down the glen. We knew who lived there, and they knew we knew. There would be no trouble from them. Just ahead of us was a ruined barn, a rectangle of collapsed drystone

walling within which rowans grew and rusty sheets of fallen corrugated iron roofing sheltered nettles and brambles.

We'd come down at the right place. A couple of hundred metres to the left, a railway bridge crossed the road at an awkward zigzag bend. The bridge had been mined the previous night; the detonation cable should be snaking back to the ruined barn. A train was due in an hour and ten minutes. Our job was to bring down the bridge, giving the train just enough time to stop – civilian casualties weren't necessary for this operation. We intended to levy a revolutionary tax on the passengers and any valuable goods in transit before turning them out on the road and sending the empty train over where the bridge had been, thus blocking the road and railway and creating an ambush chokepoint for any soldiers or cops who were sent to the scene. Booby-trapping the wreckage would be gravy, if we had the time.

I waved forward the next man behind me, and he did likewise, and one by one we all emerged from the fog and hunkered down behind the lip of a shallow gully. Andy and Gordon were there, they'd been with me since the street-fighting days in Greenock. Of the others, three – Sandy and Mike and Neil – were also from Clydeside and four were local (from our point of view – in their own eyes Ian from Strome and Murdo from Torridon and Donald from Ullapool and Norman

from Inverness were almost as distinct from each other in their backgounds as they were from ours).

'Tormod,' I said to Norman, 'you go and check out the bothy there, give us a wave if the electrician has done his job right. Two if he hasn't. Lie low and wait for the signal.'

'There's no signal.'

'The fucking whistle. My whistle.'

'Oh, right you are.'

Crouching, he ran to the ruin, and waved once after a minute. I sent Andy half a mile up the line to the nearest cutting, with a walkie-talkie, ready to confirm that the train had passed, and deployed the others on both sides of the bridge and both sides of the road. Apart from watching for any premature trouble, and being ready to raid the train when it had stopped, they were to stop any civilian vehicles that might chance to go under the bridge at the wrong moment. A light drizzle began to fall, and a front of heavier rain was marching up the glen from the west. It was still about five miles distant but with a good blow behind it, the opening breezes of which were already chilling my wet legs.

I had just settled myself and the Bren and the walkie-talkie behind a boulder on the hillside overlooking the bridge, with half an hour to spare before the train was due to pass at 12.11, when I heard the sound of a train far up the glen to the east. I couldn't see it, none of us could, except maybe Andy. I called him up.

'Passenger train,' he said. 'Wait a minute, it's got a couple of goods wagons at the back – shit, no! It's low-loaders! They're carrying two tanks!'

'Troop train,' I guessed. 'Maybe. Confirm when it passes.'

'I can check it frae here wi the glasses.'

He did, but still couldn't be certain.

Two minutes crawled by. The sound of the train filled the glen, or seemed to, until a sheep bleated nearby, startlingly loud. The radio crackled.

'Confirmed brown job,' said Andy, just as the train emerged from the cutting and into view. It wasn't travelling very fast, maybe just over twenty miles per hour.

I had a choice. I could let this one pass, and continue with the operation, or I could seize this immensely dangerous chance to wreak far more havoc than we'd planned.

I watched the train pass below me, waited until the engine had crossed the bridge, and blew the whistle. Norman didn't hesitate. The blast came when the third carriage of the train was on the bridge. It utterly failed to bring the bridge down, but it threw that carriage upwards and sideways, off the rails. It ploughed through the bridge parapet and its front end crashed on to the road. The remaining four carriages con-certina'd into its rear end. One of them rolled on to the embankment, the one behind that was derailed, and

the two tank-transporting flatbeds remained on the track.

The engine, and the two front carriages, had by this time travelled a quarter of a mile further down the track, and were accelerating rapidly away. There was nothing that could be done about that. I opened fire at once on the wreck, raking the bursts along the carriage windows. The rest of the squad followed up, then, like myself, they must have ducked down to await return fire.

In the silence that followed the crash and the firing, other noises gradually became audible. Among the screams and yells from the wreckage were the shouts of command. Within seconds a spatter of rifle and pistol fire started up. I raised my head cautiously, watched for the flashes, and directed single shots from the Bren in their direction.

Silence again. Neil and Murdo reported in on the walkie-talkie from the other side of the track, and up ahead a bit. They'd each hit one or two attempts at rescue work or flight. We seemed to have the soldiers on the train pinned down. At the same time it was difficult for us to break cover ourselves. In any sustained exchange of fire we were likely to be the first to run out of ammunition, and then to be picked off as we ran.

This impasse was brought to an end after half an hour by a torrential downpour and a further descent of the

clouds. The scheduled train, either cancelled or fore-warned, hadn't arrived. Any cars arriving at the scene had backed off and turned away, unmolested by us. We regrouped by the roadside, west of the bridge, well within earshot of the carriage that had crashed on the road.

'This is murder,' said Norman.

I was well aware of the many lives my decision had just ended or wrecked. I had no compunction about that, being even more aware of how many lives we had saved at the troops' destination.

'Seen any white flags, have you?' I snarled. 'Until you do, we're still fighting.'

'Only question is,' said Andy, 'do we pull back now while we're ahead?'

'There'll be rescue and reinforcement coming for sure,' said Murdo. 'The engine could come steaming back any minute, for one thing.'

'They're probably over-estimating us,' I said, thinking aloud in the approved democratic manner. 'I mean, who'd be mad enough to attack a troop train with ten men?'

We laughed, huddled in the pouring rain. The wind-speed was increasing by the minute.

'There'll be no air support in this muck,' said Sandy.

'All the same,' I said, 'our best bet is to pull out now we have the chance and there's nothing more to— Wait a minute. What about the tanks?'

'Can't do much damage to them,' said Mike.

'Aye,' I said, 'but think of the damage we can do *with* them.'

. . .

It was easy. It was ridiculously, pathetically, trivially easy. Four of us had National Service experience with tanks, so we split into two groups and after firing a few shots to keep the enemy's heads down we knocked the shackles off the chains and commandeered both tanks. They were fuelled and armed, ready for action. We crashed them off the sides of the flatbeds and drove them perilously down the steep slope to the road, shelled the train, drove under the bridge, shelled the train again, then shelled the bridge. Then we drove over the tracks and around the back of the now-collapsed bridge and a couple of miles up the road, and off to one side, and when the relief column arrived – a dozen troop trucks and four armoured cars – we started shelling that.

By mid-afternoon we'd inflicted hundreds of casualties and had the remaining troops and vehicles completely pinned down. Reinforcements from our side began to arrive, pouring fire from the ridges into the glen, raiding more weapons and ammunition from the train and the relief column; and then attacking *its* relief column. The battle of Glen Carron was turning into the biggest engagement of the war in the British Isles. The increas-

ingly appalling weather was entirely to our advantage, although my squad, at least, were on the point of pneumonia from the soaking we'd got earlier.

The first we knew of the bomber's arrival was when we lost contact with the men on the ridge. A minute later, I saw through the periscope the other tank – a few hundred metres away at the time – take a direct hit. That erupting flash of earth and metal told me without a doubt that Gordon was dead, along with Ian, Mike, Sandy and Norman.

'Reverse reverse reverse!' I shouted.

Murdo slammed us into reverse gear and hit the accelerator, throwing me painfully forward as we shot up a slope and into a birch-screened gully. The tank lurched upward as the bomb missed us by about twenty metres, then crashed back down on its tracks.

Blood poured from my brow and lip.

'Everybody all right?' I yelled.

No reply. Silence. I looked down and saw Andy tugging my leg, mouthing and nodding. He pointed to his ears. I grimaced acknowledgement and looked again through the periscope and saw the bomber descend towards the road just across the glen from us, by one of the trapped columns. Five hundred metres away, and exactly level with us.

There was a shell in the chamber. I swivelled the turret and racked the gun as hearing returned through a raging ringing in my ears, just in time to be deafened

again as I fired. My aim was by intuition, with no use of the sights, pure Zen like a perfect throw of a stone. I knew it was going to hit, and it did.

The bomber shot upwards, skimmed towards us, then fluttered down to settle athwart the river at the bottom of the glen, just fifty metres away and ten metres below us, lying there like a fucking enormous landmine in our path.

I poked Murdo's shoulder with my foot and he engaged the forward gear. Andy set up a bit of suppressing fire with the machine-gun. We slewed to a halt beside the bomber. I grabbed a Bren, threw open the hatch and clambered through and jumped down. My ears were still ringing. The wind was fierce, the rain an instant skin-soaking, the wind-chill terrible. Water poured off the bomber like sea off a surfacing submarine. There was a smell of peat-bog and metal and crushed myrtle. Smoke drifted from a ragged notch in its edge, similar to the one on the crippled bomber I'd seen all those years ago.

I walked around the bomber, warily leaping past the snouts of machine-guns in its rim. With the Bren's butt I banged the hatch. The thing rang like a bell, even louder than my tinnitus.

The hatch opened. I stood back and levelled the Bren. A big visored helmet emerged, then long arms levered up a torso, and then the hips and legs swung up and out. The pilot slid down the side of the bomber and

stood in front of me, arms raised high. Very slowly, the hands went to the helmet and lifted it off.

A cascade of blonde hair shook loose. The pilot was incredibly beautiful and she was about seven feet tall.

· · ·

We left the tank sabotaged and blocking the road about five miles to the west, and took off into the hills. Through the storm and the gathering dusk we struggled to a lonely safe house, miles from anywhere. Our prisoner was tireless and silent. Her flying-suit was dark green and black, to all appearances standard for an American pilot, right down to the badges. She carried her helmet and knotted her hair deftly at her nape. Her Colt .45 and Bowie knife she surrendered without protest.

The safe house was a gamekeeper's lodge, with a kitchen and a couple of rooms, the larger of which had a fireplace. Dry wood was stacked on the hearth. We started the fire and stripped off our wet clothes – all of our clothes – and hung them about the place, then one by one we retrieved dry clothes from the stash in the back room. The prisoner observed us without a blink, and removed her own flying-suit. Under it she was wearing a closer-fitting garment of what looked like woven aluminium, with tubes running under its surface. It covered a well-proportioned female body. Too well-proportioned, indeed, for the giant she was. She

sprawled on the worn armchair by the fire and looked at us, still silent, and carefully untied her wet hair and let it fall down her back.

Murdo, Andy, Neil and Donald huddled in front of the fire. I stood behind them, holding the prisoner's pistol.

'Donald,' I said, 'you take the first look-out. You'll find oilskins in the back. Neil, make some tea, and give it to Donald first.'

'Three sugars, if we have it,' said Donald, getting up and padding through to the other room. Neil disappeared into the kitchen. Sounds of him fiddling with and cursing the little gas stove followed. The prisoner smiled, for the first time. Her pale features were indeed beautiful, but somewhat angular, almost masculine; her eyes were a distinct violet, and very large.

'Talk,' I told her.

'Jodelle Smith,' she said. 'Flight-Lieutenant. Serial number . . .' She rattled it off.

The voice was deep, for a woman, but soft, the American accent perfect. Donald gave her a baleful glare as he headed for the door and the storm outside it.

'All right,' I said. 'We are not signatories to the Geneva Convention. We do not regard you as a prisoner of war, but as a war criminal, an air pirate. You have one chance of being treated as a prisoner of war, with all the rights that go with that, and that is to answer all our questions. Otherwise, we will turn you

over to the nearest revolutionary court. They're pretty biblical around here. They'll probably stone you to death.'

I don't know how the lads kept a straight face through all that. Perhaps it was the anger and grief over the loss of our friends and comrades, the same feeling that came out in my own voice. I could indeed have wished her dead, but otherwise I was bluffing – there were no revolutionary courts in the region, and anyway our policy with prisoners was to disarm them, attempt to interrogate them, and turn them loose as soon as it was safe to do so.

The pilot sat silent for a moment, head cocked slightly to one side, then shrugged and smiled.

'Other bomber pilots have been captured,' she said. 'They've all been recovered unharmed.' She straightened up in the chair, and leaned forward. 'If you're not satisfied with the standard name, rank, and serial number, I'm happy to talk to you about anything other than military secrets. What would you like to know?'

I glanced at the others. I had never shared my father's story, or my own, with any of them, and I was glad of that now because the appearance of this pilot would have discredited it. Compared with what my father had described, she looked human. Compared with most people, she looked very strange.

'Where do you really come from?' I asked.

'Venus,' she said.

The others all laughed. I didn't.

'What happened to the other kind of pilots?' I asked. I held out one hand about a metre above the ground, as though patting a child's head.

'Oh, we took over from the Martians a long time ago,' she told us earnestly. 'They're still involved in the war, of course, but they're not on the front line any more. The Americans found their appearance disconcerting, and concealing them became too much of a hassle.'

I glared down the imminent interruptions from my men.

'You're saying there are two alien species fighting on the American side?'

'Yes,' she said. She laughed suddenly. 'Greys are from Mars, blondes are from Venus.'

'Total fucking *cac*,' said Neil. 'She's a Yank. They're always tall. Better food.'

'Maybe she is,' I said, 'but she is not the kind of pilot I was expecting. And I've seen one of the other kind. My father saw it up close.'

The woman's eyebrows went up.

'The Aird incident? 1964?'

I nodded.

'Ah,' she said. 'Your father must be . . . Dr Malcolm Donald Matheson, and you are his son, John.'

'How the hell do you know that?'

'I've read the reports.'

'This is insane,' said Andy. 'It's some kind of trick, it's

a trap. We shouldnae say another word, or listen tae any.'

'There's eggs and bacon and tatties in the kitchen,' I said. 'See if you can make yourself useful.'

He glowered at me and stalked out.

'But he's right, you know,' I said, loud enough for Andy to overhear. 'We are going to have to send you up a level or two, for interrogation, as soon as the storm passes. Will you still talk then?'

She spread her hands. 'On the same basis as I've spoken to you, yes. No military secrets.'

'Aye, just disinformation,' said Murdo. 'You're not telling us that it wouldn't be a military secret if the Yanks really were getting help from *outer space*? But making people believe it, now, that would be worth something. Christ, it's enough of a job fighting the Americans. Who would fight the fucking Martians?'

He leaned back and laughed harshly.

The woman who called herself Jodelle gazed at him with narrowed, thoughtful eyes.

'There is that argument,' she said. 'There is the other argument, that if the Communists could claim the real enemy was not human they would unite even more people against the Allied side, and that the same know-ledge would create all kinds of problems – political, religious, philosophical – for Allied morale. So far, the latter argument has prevailed.'

My grip tightened on the pistol.

'You are talking about psychological warfare,' I said. 'And you are doing it, right here, now. Shut the fuck up.'

She gave us a pert smile and shrugged.

'No more talking to her,' I said.

My own curiosity was burning me inside, but I knew that to pursue the conversation – with the mood here as it was – really would be demoralising and confusing. I got everybody busy guarding the prisoner, cleaning weapons, laying the table. Andy brought through plates laden with steaming, fragrant thick bacon and fried eggs and boiled potatoes. I relieved Donald on the outside watch before taking a bite myself, and prowled around in the howling wet dark with my M-16 under the oilskin cape and my belly grumbling. The window blinds were keeping the light in all right, and only the wind-whipped smoke from the chimney could betray our presence. I kept my closest attention to downwind, where someone might smell it. There was no chance of anyone seeing it.

I was looking that way, peering and listening intently through the dark to the east, when I felt a prickle in the back of my neck and smelled something electric.

I turned with a sort of reluctance, as though expecting to see a ghost. What I saw was a bomber, haloed in blue, descending between me and the house. There might have been a fizzing sound, or that may be just a memory of the hissing rain. For a moment I stood as still

as the bomber, which floated preternaturally above the ground. Then I raised the rifle. Something flashed out from the bomber, and I was knocked backwards, and senseless.

. . .

I woke to voices, and pain. My skin smarted all over; my eyelids hurt to open. I was lying on my side on a slightly yielding smooth grey floor. The light was pearly and sourceless. Moving slightly, I found I had some bruises and what felt like scrapes on my back, but apart from that and the burning feeling everything seemed to be fine. My oilskins were gone, as were my weapons and, curiously enough, my watch. I raised my head, propped myself on one elbow and looked around. The room I lay in was circular, about fifteen metres across. My comrades were lying beside me, unconscious, looking sunburned, but breathing normally and apparently uninjured. There was a sort of bench or shelf around the room, which in one section looped away from the wall to form a seat, at which a tall person with long fair hair sat facing away from me, hands on a pair of knobbed levers. Other parts of the shelf were not padded seating but tables and odd panels. Above the bench was a black screen or window which likewise encircled the room.

Sitting on the bench, on either side of the person I guessed was the pilot, were three similar people – one

of them, just then noticing that I was stirring, being the woman we'd captured – and a small creature with a large head, slit mouth, tiny nostrils and enormous black eyes. Its skin was grey, but somehow not an unhealthy grey – it had a glow to it, a visible warmth underneath; though hairless it reminded me of the skin of a seal. Its legs were short, its arms long, and its hands – I recalled my father's words, and felt a slight thrill at their confirmation – bore four long digits.

It too noticed me, and it looked directly at me and – it didn't blink, something flicked sideways across its eyes, like an eagle's. The woman stood up and stepped over and stood looking down at me.

'There's no need to be afraid of the Martian,' she said.

'I'm not afraid,' I said, then caught myself. 'John Matheson, unit commander, MB 246.'

She reached down, took my hand and hauled me to my feet, without effort. There was something wrong about my weight. I felt curiously light.

'Your friends will wake up shortly,' she said. 'OK, consider yourself a prisoner of war if you like, but there's no need to not be civil. We have nothing to hide from you any more, and there really isn't anything we want to find out from you.'

I said nothing. She pointed to the bench.

'Relax,' she said, 'sit down, have a coffee.' Then she giggled, in a very disarming way. ' "For you, Johnny, the vor iss over." '

Her fake, Ealing-studio German accent was as perfect as her genuine-sounding American one. I couldn't forbear to smile back, and walked over to the seat. On the way I stumbled a little. It was like the top step that isn't there.

'Martian gravity,' Jodelle said, steadying me. The Martian bowed his big head slightly, as though in apology. I sat down beside one of the other people, the 'Venusians' as I perforce mentally labelled them. All except Jodelle were evidently male, though their hair was as long and fair as hers. One of them passed me a mug of coffee; out of the corner of my eye, I noticed a coffee pot and electric kettle on one of the table sections, and some mugs and, banally enough, a kilogramme packet of Tate & Lyle sugar.

'My name is Soren,' the man said. He waved towards the others. 'The pilot is Olaf, and the man next to him is Harold.'

'And my name is Chuck,' said the Martian. His small shoulders shrugged. 'That's what I'm called around here, anyway.' His voice was like that of a tough wee boy, his accent American, but he sounded like he was speaking a learned second language.

I nodded at them all and said nothing, gratefully sipping the coffee. Outside, the view was completely black, though the movements of the pilot's eyes, head, and hands appeared to be responding to some visible exterior environment.

One by one, Neil, Donald, Murdo and Andy came round, and went through the same process of disorientation, astonishment, reassurance and suspicion as I had. We ended up sitting together, not speaking to each other or to our captors, perhaps silently mourning the loss of our comrades and friends in the other tank. The bomber's crew talked amongst themselves in a language I did not recognise, and attended to instruments. None of us was in anything but a hostile mood, and if the aliens had been less unknown in their intentions and capabilities we might have regarded their evident lack of concern as an opportunity to try to overwhelm them, rather than – as we tacitly acknowledged – evidence that they had no reason to fear us.

After about half an hour, they relaxed, and all sat down on the long seat.

'Almost there,' Jodelle Smith said.

Before any of us could respond, one side of the encircling window filled with the glare of the sun, instantly dimmed by some property of the display; the other with the light of that same sun reflected on white clouds, of which I glimpsed a dazzling, visibly curved expanse a second before we plunged into them. Moments later we were underneath them, and a green surface spread below us. Looking up, I could see the silvery underside of the clouds. Our rapid descent soon brought the green surface into focus as an apparently endless forest, broken by lakes and rivers, and by plateaus or gentler rises

covered with grass. After a few seconds we were low enough for the shadow of the bomber to be visible, skimming across the treetops. The circle of shade enlarged, and then disappeared. I blinked, and saw that we were now stationary above a broad valley bounded by high sandstone cliffs and divided by a wide, meandering river.

Then, with a yawing motion which we could see but not feel – so it seemed that the landscape swayed, and not the ship – we descended, and settled on a grassy plain. Around us, in the middle distance, were rows of Nissen huts; in the farther distance, watchtowers and barbed wire.

'Welcome to Venus,' said the pilot.

• • •

The camp held about a thousand people, from all over the world. Most of them were Front soldiers or cadre. There were as many women as there were men, and there were some children. The Front basically ran the camp, through committees of the various national sections, and an international committee for which the main qualification seemed to be fluency in Russian. The only rule that the Venusians enforced was a curfew and blackout between sunset and sunrise. They didn't bother about which hut you spent the night in, so long as you were in a hut.

They gave us no work to do, and watched uncon-

cerned as we practised drill and unarmed combat, sweltering in the heat and humidity. Food and drink were adequate, and in fact more varied and nutritious than the fare to which most of the inmates, including myself, had become accustomed. This is not to say that our confinement was pleasant. The continuous cloud cover felt like a great shining lid pressing down on us, day after day. Every day it seemed to, or perhaps actually did, descend a little lower. The nightly lock-downs were hellish, even though the huts did in fact cool down somewhat. The wire around the camp was almost equally suffocating, although we'd realised that it wasn't so much there to keep us in as to keep the dinosaurs out. The same was true of the guards' strange weapons, which could – if turned to a much higher setting than was ever used against prisoners – fire bolts of electricity or plasma sufficient to turn back even the biggest of the great blundering beasts which flocked to the river every couple of days, their feet making the plain shake. We called them dinosaurs, because they resembled the reconstructions of dinosaurs which most of us had seen in books, but I knew from my scientific education that they could not be dinosaurs – they were too vigorous, too obviously hot-blooded, to be the sluggish reptilian giants of the Triassic and Jurassic eras. Whatever they may have been, their presence certainly discouraged attempts to escape.

The British contingent was in two Nissen huts: twenty men in one, twenty women in the other. They had a committee of three men, three women, and a chairman, and they spent a lot of time trying to regulate sexual relations. It was all very British and messy, uncomfortably between the strict puritanism of the Chinese comrades and the easy-going, if occasionally violent, mores of the Latin Americans and Africans. My unit decided to ignore all that and do what we considered the proper British thing.

We set up an escape committee.

• • •

'What the hell are you doing, Matheson?'

I waved my free hand. 'Just a minute—'

It didn't interrupt my counting. When I'd finished, I put the one-metre line and the 250-gramme tin of peas on the table and glanced over my calculations before looking up at Purdie. The young Englishman was on our hut committee and the camp committee, but not the escape committee, which he regarded as a diversion in both senses of the word.

'We're not on Venus,' I said.

He glanced over his shoulder, as if to confirm that we were still alone in the hut, then sat on a corner of the table.

'How d'you figure that out?'

'Pendulum swing,' I said. 'Galileo's experiment. The

gravity here is exactly the same as on Earth. Venus has about eighty per cent of the mass of Earth.'

'H'mm,' he said. 'Well done. Most people begin by wondering why nothing feels lighter, and then put it down to our muscles adapting to the supposed lower gravity. Still, can't say it's a surprise, old chap. Some of us reckon they keep us in at night because if we went outside we could see the moon through the cloud cover, and even the least educated of us is aware that Venus doesn't *have* a bloody moon.'

'So where are we?' I waved a hand. 'It seems a wee bit out of the way, if this is Earth.'

He crooked one leg over the other and lit a cigarette.

'Well, the camp committee has considered that. The usual explanation is that we're in some unexplored region of a South American jungle, something like what's-his-name's *The Lost World*.'

'Conan Doyle,' I said automatically. I screwed up my eyes against the smoke and the glaring light from the open door of the hut. 'Doesn't seem likely to me.'

'Me neither,' said Purdie cheerfully. 'For one thing, the midday sun isn't high enough in the sky for this to be a tropical latitude, but it's *bloody* hot. Any other ideas?'

'What if instead we're in somewhere out of *The Time Machine*? Well, you know . . . *dinosaurs*?'

Purdie frowned and probed in his ear with a finger.

'That has come up. Our Russian comrades shot it

down in flames. Time travel is ruled out by dialectical materialism, I gather. But I must say, this place does strike me as frightfully Cretaceous, the anomaly of hot-blooded dinosaurs aside. My personal theory is that we're on a planet around another star, which resembles Earth in the Cretaceous period.'

He cracked a smile. 'That, however, implies a vastly more advanced civilization which either isn't Communist or *is* Communist and fights on the side of the imperialists. Neither of which are acceptable speculations to the, ah, leading comrades here, who thus stick with the line that the self-styled Venusians and Martians are the spawn of Nazi medical experiments, or some such.'

'Bollocks,' I said.

Purdie shrugged. 'You may well say that, but I wouldn't. I myself am troubled by the thought that my own theory at least strongly suggests – even if it doesn't, strictly speaking, require – faster-than-light travel, which is ruled out by Einstein – an authority who to me carries more weight on matters of physics than Engels or Lenin, I'm afraid.'

'Relativity doesn't rule out time travel,' I said. 'Even if dialectical materialism does.'

'And no science whatever rules out lost-world relict dinosaur populations,' said Purdie. He shrugged. 'Occam's razor and all that, keeps up morale, so lost world is the official line.'

'First I've heard of it,' I said. 'Nobody's even suggested we're not on Venus in the two weeks I've been here.'

'Bit of a test, comrade,' he said dryly. He stubbed out his cigarette, hopped off the table and stuck out his right hand for me to shake. 'Congratulations on passing it. Now, how would you like to join the *real* escape committee?'

. . .

The official escape committee had long since worked through and discarded the laughable expedients – tunnels, gliders and so on – which I and my mates, perhaps over-influenced by such tales of derring-do as *The Colditz Story* and *The Wooden Horse*, had earnestly evaluated. The only possibility was for a mass break-out, exploiting the only factor of vulnerability we could see in the camp's defences, and one which itself was implicitly part of them: the dinosaur herds. It would also exploit the fact that, as far as we knew, the guards were reluctant to use lethal force on prisoners. So far, at least, they'd only ever turned on us the kind of electrical shock which had knocked out me and my team, and indeed most people here at the time of their capture or subsequent resistance.

The tedious details of how a prison-camp escape attempt is prepared have been often enough recounted in the genre of POW memoirs referred to above, and need not be repeated here. Suffice it to say that about

fifty days after my arrival, the preparations were complete. From then on, all those involved in the scheme waited hourly for the approach of a suitably large herd, and on the second day of our readiness, conveniently soon after breakfast, one arrived.

About a score of the great beasts: bulls, cows, and calves, their tree-trunk-thick legs striding across the plain, their tree-top-high heads swaying to sniff and stooping to browse, were marching straight towards the eastern fence of the camp, which lay athwart their route to the river. The guards were just bestirring themselves to rack up the setting on their plasma rifles when the riot started.

At the western end of the camp a couple of Chinese women started screaming, and on this cue scores of other prisoners rushed to surround them and pile in to a highly realistic and noisy fight. Guards from the perimeter patrol raced towards them, and were immediately turned on and overwhelmed by a further crowd that just kept on coming, leaping or stepping over those who'd fallen to the low-level electric blasts. At that the guards from the watchtowers on that side began to descend, some of them firing.

My team was set for the actual escape, not the diversion. I was crouched behind the door of our hut with Murdo, Andy, Neil, Donald and a dozen others, including Purdie. We'd grabbed our stashed supplies and our improvised tools, and now awaited our chance.

Another human wave assault, this time a crowd of Russians heading for the fence where the guards were belatedly turning to face the oncoming dinosaurs, thundered past. We dashed out behind them and ran for an empty food-delivery truck, temporarily un-guarded. It even had a plasma-rifle, which I instantly commandeered, racked inside.

The Russians swarmed up the wire, standing on each other's shoulders like acrobats. The guards, trying to deal with them and the dinosaurs, failed to cope with both. A bull dinosaur brought down the fence and two watchtowers, and by the time he'd been himself laid low with concerted plasma fire, we'd driven over the remains of the fence and hordes of prisoners were fleeing in every direction.

Within minutes the first bombers arrived, skimming low, rounding up the escapees. They missed us, perhaps because they'd mistaken the truck – a very standard US Army Dodge – for one of their own. We abandoned it at the foot of the cliffs, scaled them in half an hour of frantic scrambling up corries and chimneys, and by the time the bombers came looking for us we'd disappeared into the trees.

. . .

Heat, damp, thorns, and very large dragonflies. Apart from that last and the small dinosaur-like animals – some, to our astonishment, with feathers – scuttling

through the undergrowth, the place didn't look like another planet, or even the remote past. Since my knowledge of what the remote past was supposed to look like was derived entirely from dim memories of *Look and Learn* and slightly fresher memories of a stroll through the geological wing of the Hunterian Museum, Glasgow, this wasn't saying much. I vaguely expected giant ferns and cycads and so forth, and found perfectly recognisable conifers, oaks and maples. The flowers were less instantly recognisable, but didn't look particularly primitive, or exotic.

I shared these thoughts with Purdie, who laughed.

'You're thinking of the Carboniferous, old chap,' he said. 'This is all solidly Cretaceous, so far.'

'Could be modern,' I said.

'Apart from the animals,' he pointed out, as though this wasn't obvious. 'And as I said, it's not tropical, but it's too bloody hot to be a temperate latitude.'

I glanced back. Our little column was plodding along behind us. We were heading in an approximately upward direction, on a reasonably gentle slope.

'I've thought about this,' I said. 'What if this whole area is some kind of artificial reserve in *North* America? If it's possible to genetically . . . engineer, I suppose would be the word . . . different kinds of humans, why shouldn't it be possible to do the same with birds and lizards and so on, and make a sort of botched copy of dinosaurs?'

'And keep it all under some vast artificial cloud canopy?' He snorted. 'You over-estimate the imperialists, let alone the Nazi scientists, comrade.'

'Maybe we're under a huge dome,' I said, not entirely seriously. I looked up at the low sky, which seemed barely higher than the tree-tops. It really had become lower since we'd arrived. 'Buckminster Fuller had plans that were no less ambitious than that.'

Purdie wiped sweat from his forehead with the back of his hand. 'Now that,' he said, 'is quite a plausible suggestion. It sure *feels* like we're in a bloody greenhouse. Mind you, none of us saw anything like that from the bomber.'

'That was a screen, not a window.'

'Hmm. A remarkably realistic screen, in that case. Back to implausibly advanced technology.'

We wouldn't have to speculate for long, because our course was taking us directly up to the cloud level, which we reached within an hour or so. I assigned my lads the task of guiding the others, who were quite unfamiliar with the techniques of low-visibility walking, and we all headed on up. First wisps then dense damp billows of fog surrounded us. I led the way and moved forward cautiously, whistling signals back and forth. Behind me I could just see Purdie and two of the English women comrades. Underfoot the ground became grassier, and around us the trees became shorter and the bushes more sparse. The only way to

follow a particular direction was to go upslope, and that
– with a few inevitable wrong turnings that led us into
declivities – we did.

The fog thinned. Clutching the plasma rifle, hoping
I had correctly figured out how to use it, I walked
forward and up and into clear air. A breeze blew
refreshingly into my face, and as I glanced back I saw
that it had pushed back the fog and revealed all of our
straggling party. We were on one of the wide, rounded
hilltops I'd seen from the bomber. In the far distance I
could see other green islands above the clouds. The sky
was blue, the sun was bright.

All around us, people rose out of the long grass,
aiming plasma rifles. I dropped mine and raised my
hands.

About a hundred metres in front of us was the wire
fence of another camp.

• • •

We went into the camp without resistance, but without being searched or, in my case, disarmed: I was told
to pick up my rifle and sling it over my shoulder. The
people were human beings like us, but they were
weird. They spoke English, in strange accents and
with a lot of unfamiliar words. Several of them were
coloured or half-caste, but their accents were as
English as those of the rest. I found myself walking
beside a young woman with part of her hair dyed

violet. I knew it was a dye because it was growing out: the roots were black. She had several rings and studs in her ear, and not just in the earlobe. She was wearing baggy grey trousers with pockets at the thighs, and a silky scarlet sleeveless top with a silver patch shaped like a rabbit. Around her bicep was a tattoo of thorns. Under her tarty make-up her face was quite attractive. Her teeth looked amazingly white and even, like an American's.

'My name's Tracy,' she said. She had some kind of Northern English accent; I couldn't place it more than that. 'You?'

Name, rank, serial number . . .

'Where you from?'

Name, rank, serial number . . .

'Forget that,' she said. 'You're not a prisoner.'

A massive gate made from logs and barbed wire was being pushed shut behind us. Nissen huts inside a big square of fence, a bomber parked just outside it.

'Oh no?' I said.

'Keeps the fucking dinosaurs out, dunnit?'

Somebody handed me a tin mug of tea, black with a lot of sugar. I sipped it and looked around. If this was a camp it was one where prisoners had guns. Or one run by trusties . . . I was still suspicious.

'Where are the aliens?' I asked.

'The what?'

'The Venusians, the Martians . . .' I held my free hand above my head, then at chest height.

Tracy laughed, 'Is that what they told you?'

I nodded. 'Not sure if I believe them, though.'

She was still chuckling. 'You lot must be from Commie World. Never built the rockets, right?'

'The Russians have rockets,' I said with some indignation. 'The biggest in the world – they have a range of hundreds of kilometres!'

'Exactly. No ICBMs.' She smiled at my frown. 'Inter-Continental Ballistic Missiles. None of them, and no space-probes. Jeez. You could still half-believe this might be Venus, with jungles and tall Aryans. And that the Greys are Martians.'

'Well, what are they?' I asked, becoming irritated by her smug teasing.

'Time travellers,' she said. 'From the future.' She shivered slightly. 'From *another* world's future. The ones you call the Venusians are from about half a million years up ahead of the twentieth century, the Greys're from maybe five million. In your world's twentieth century they fly bombers and fight Commies. In mine they're just responsible for flying saucers, alien abductions, cattle mutilations and odd sock phenomena.'

I let this incomprehensibly pass.

'So where are we now?'

I meant the camp. I knew where we were in general, but that was what she answered.

'This Johnny-boy, is the past. They can never go back to the same future, but they can go back to the same place in the past, where they can make no difference. The common past, the past of us all – the Cretaceous.'

She looked at me with a bit more sympathy. My companions were finishing off their tea and gazing around, looking as baffled and edgy as I felt. The other prisoners, if that was what they were, gathered around us seemed more alien than the bomber pilots.

'Come on,' Tracy said, gesturing towards some rows of seats in front of which a table had been dragged. 'Debriefing time. You have a lot to learn.'

. . .

I have learned a lot.

I tug the reins and the big Clydesdale turns, and as I follow the plough around I see a porpoise leap in the choppy water of the Moray Firth. My hands and back are sore but I'm getting used to it, and the black soil here is rich, and arable after the trees have been cut down and their stumps dynamited. The erratic boulders have been cleared away long ago, by the long-dead first farmers of this land, and no glaciers have revisited it since its last farmers passed away. The rougher ground is pasture, grazed by half-wild long-horns, a rugged synthetic species. The village is stockaded on a hilltop nearby. We have no human enemies, but wolves, bears and lions prowl the forests and moors. We are not

barbarians – the plough that turns the furrow I walk has an iron blade, and the revolver on my hip was made in Hartford, Connecticut, millennia ago and worlds away. The post-humans settled us – and other colonies – on this empty Earth with machinery and medicines, weapons and tools and libraries, and enough partly-used ball-point pens to keep us all scribbling until our descendants can make their own.

On countless other empty Earths they have done the same. Somewhere unreachable, but close to hand, another man, perhaps another John Matheson, may be tramping a slightly different furrow. I wish him well.

There are many possible worlds, and in almost all of them humanity didn't survive the time from which most of us have been taken. Either the United States and the Soviet Union destroyed each other and the rest of civilisation in an atomic war in the fifties or sixties, or they didn't, and the collapse of the socialist states in the late twentieth century so discredited socialism and international co-operation that humanity failed utterly to unite in time to forestall the environmental disasters of the twenty-first.

In a few, a very few possible worlds, enough scattered remnants of humanity survived as savages to eventually – hundreds of thousands of years later – become the ancestors of the post-human species we called the Venusians. Who in turn – millions of years later – themselves gave rise to the post-human species we

called the Martians. It was the latter who discovered time travel, and with it some deep knowledge about the future and past of the universe.

I don't pretend to understand it. As Feynmann said – in a world where he didn't die in jail – it all goes back to the experiment with the light and the two slits, and Feynmann himself didn't pretend to understand *that*. What we have been told is simply this – that the past of the universe, its very habitability for human beings, depends on its future being one – or rather, many – which contain as many human beings and their successors as possible, until the end of time.

It is not enough for the time-travellers to intervene in histories such as the one from which I come, and by defeating Communism while avoiding atomic war, save a swathe of futures for co-operation and survival. They also have to repopulate the time-lines in which humanity destroyed itself, and detonate new shock-waves of possibility that will spread humanity across time and forward through it, on an ever-expanding, widening front.

The big mare stops and looks at me, and whinnies. The sun is low above the hills to the west, the hills where I once – or many times – fought. Its light is red in the sky. The dust from the last atomic war is no longer dangerous, but it will linger in the high atmosphere for thousands of years to come.

I unharness the horse, heave the plough to the shed

at the end of the field, and lead the beast up the hill towards the village. The atomic generator is humming, the lights are coming on, and dinner in the communal kitchen will soon be ready. Tracy will be putting away the day's books in the library, and yawning and stretching herself. Maybe this evening, after we've all eaten, she can be persuaded to tell us some stories. For me she has many fascinations – she's quite unlike any woman I've ever met – and the only one I'm happy for her to share with everybody else is her stories from the world where, I still feel, history turned out almost as it would have done without any meddling at all by the time-travellers: her world, the world where the prototype bomber didn't work; the world where, as she puts it, the Roswell saucer crashed.